My Plan B

Middlemarch Shifters 11

Shelley Munro

My Plan B

Copyright © 2023 by Shelley Munro

Print ISBN: 978-1-99-106314-4
Digital ISBN: 978-0-473-37048-0

Editor: Mary Moran

Cover: Kim Killion, The Killion Group

Munro Press, New Zealand.

First Munro Press electronic publication October 2016

First Munro Press print publication February 2023

For Paul.

INTRODUCTION

PLAN A SUCKS. MOVE over for plan B...

Sports commentator and reporter, Megan Saxon, has it all. The perfect career and freedom to do anything she wants, but as the years creep by she realizes love, or at least male companionship, has thumbed its nose at her. With the help of her agent-friend, she hatches Plan B. A brief love affair with a younger man will cure all ills and help her plan for the future.

The problem with plan B? Nothing, I repeat *nothing*, goes the way she plans, and she's left gasping for breath, dodging reporters and suffering acute embarrassment.

The. Worst. Blushing. Epidemic. Ever.

Long-term widower and werewolf, Jacey Anderson, has moved to small country town Middlemarch to be near his grieving adult stepson, Henry, and to embrace the wide, open spaces with his wolf. He's not expecting romance and especially with a public figure who attracts reporters like flies at a dung heap. His attraction to the sexy, sassy Megan has disaster written all over it, yet try telling that to his moonstruck wolf.

Yes, this Plan B has potential calamity for both parties. A pity that neither of them has a lick of good sense when they're in the same room, touching... Kissing... Caressing...

Contains werewolves, feline shifters, and creatures that howl at the night moon. There is also hot love, laughter, and lots of teasing.

CHAPTER ONE

AUCKLAND, NEW ZEALAND

"YOU WANTED TO SEE me?"

Something was up with her boss. Megan Saxon watched Jeremy squirm in his executive chair, his gaze skittering over the sheaf of papers in front of him, over the signed and framed All Blacks jersey on the wall to her right, over the office-size basketball hoop in the left corner of his office. Finally, his gaze alighted on a pen. He seized the silver writing utensil. His fingers squeezed, and his tanned face held a wealth of frustration. Regret.

It was this last emotion that set her belly swirling with dread. Megan forced herself to stay still, to wait while her quick breakfast of milky coffee and a banana churned in her gut. Normally, Jeremy perched on the edge of his giant desk, his easy manner making her job as a sports broadcaster and journalist fun and fulfilling. Exciting. Exhilarating.

This was something else.

His garish tie—today's version covered with yellow cartoon characters—didn't stir her normal urge for wisecracks and insults. *Great*. Now Jeremy's weird mood had transferred to her.

Enough. Megan straightened on the unpadded chair—uncomfortable on purpose because Jeremy didn't favor long meetings—and cleared her throat.

Jeremy's gaze shot from his pen to her, and this time he frowned, upping her anxiety.

"What's wrong, boss?" She scrutinized the play of emotions in him and leapt to her feet, unable to remain stoic and businesslike for an instant longer. "Is it about the new sports show? I thought everything was ready for the first episode next month. I'm excited at the opportunity to work with Dallas Jones." And how! Every time she pictured the retired All Black, she did a mental *cha-cha-cha*. Her anxiety seeped away, and buoyed by this exciting career move, she didn't pace as she'd intended. Wait until she caught up with her sister and told her the official news. Rumors had floated around for months, but she hadn't been able to confirm them. "Have the big bosses decided on the final format?"

"Yes. No," Jeremy spluttered, displaying none of his usual decisiveness.

"Are you sick?" Megan pressed her lips together. Her breakfast spun another circuit of her stomach, and she swiped clammy hands down her jeans-clad thighs. "Is there a problem?"

"You're too old," Jeremy blurted.

"What?" Indignation stabbed her, stabbed her with a rusty knife. "I'm thirty-eight! Since when is that old?" She lied, deducting five years without a blink as she planted hands on her hips and glared at the insult. Damn it, she didn't look her age. Everyone said so.

"The bosses are going with Rowena Johnson as the co-host."

What? *No*. Every muscle in her body tensed. "Rowena? But she doesn't have the experience to co-anchor a sports show. She's a glorified weathergirl." Younger. Blonde. Sexy. And now she'd wrested Megan's dream job from her. No, she didn't believe it. Sudden enlightenment occurred. "Oh! I get it. You're pranking me. Good one, boss. You really got me."

"I'm not joking. Here…" He rifled through his pile of papers and handed her an inter-office memo. The official kind deemed important enough for a paper and an electronic copy.

With a noticeably trembling hand, she accepted the page and scanned the contents. Horror pinched her lips together as she groped through her confusion. "I don't understand. Are they firing me?" Her voice shook with the beginnings of anger and she blinked because tears had her vision blurring. She didn't do girly tears and prided herself on the fact. The feminine weapon had no business entering the workplace. "Are they sacking me because I'm too old?"

"No. No of course not," Jeremy snapped. "That would be illegal. In fact, I have an assignment for you." He pulled another page from the pile of papers in front of him. "Ah, yes. Here it is." He handed her a single page. "This is a weekend gig. Commentator for a Sevens rugby tournament and a general interest piece on the small town where the tournament is taking place."

Megan's brows scrunched together. "Middlemarch? I've never heard of the place."

"It's in the South Island, not far from Dunedin."

"Dunedin? It snows there." Heck, now she sounded like a whining child. "It feels as if you're sending me away. Banishing me." Her mind weighed up everything, and she shot him a glare. "What happens after this assignment? It's only one weekend. You've replaced me on the commentary team. What's next?"

Jeremy's gaze went AWOL again, refusing to meet hers. "Aw, well...that's up in the air right now."

"Up in the air?" The words emerged a smidgeon short of a shriek. Megan winced, sucked in a calming breath and clenched her fists to center herself. Once she was certain of her ability to speak, she glanced at Jeremy. "The management are shifting me sideways because of my age, because I'm a female."

"No, that's not what's happening." Once again, Jeremy's gaze didn't linger, flitting in the manner of a flighty bird scared of the neighborhood cat.

But it was happening, and both of them knew it.

A fresh surge of moisture stung her eyes. She couldn't cry in front of Jeremy. She refused to cry in a place where her male colleagues might witness her breakdown and gossip like elderly ladies in a teashop. The tittle-tattle would be bad enough without her adding fuel to their hearsay fire.

"I'll do the Middlemarch job and take a week's leave. I'd appreciate it if you inform me of my future options on my return." Megan forced the words past the lump constricting her throat and willed the pending tears to disperse. *A few more minutes.* She'd hold herself together for a few more minutes.

"Of course." Jeremy looked happier at her suggestion. "That's a good idea. I'll get Ruby to organize the tickets and accommodation. The tournament will be for three nights since the opening game is Friday night. Actually, go a day earlier and see the sights. You'll need a rental car too."

Megan nodded, unable to utter another word without falling apart. She turned away and concentrated on walking instead of running out of Jeremy's office. She left without a farewell or her usual cheek. Another word, just one utterance, might snap her grip on her emotions. This wasn't fair. She wasn't old. Since when did forty equate to a person on the scrapheap?

Anger burned as she strode through the main office. She waved when a group of her coworkers hailed her and pointed at her watch as if she were late for an appointment.

They—all men—were in their late thirties and forties. Eric was fifty-two. None of them got shunted aside because of their age. A sharp pain in her hand made her realize she'd clenched her fists hard enough for her nails to pierce the skin.

The pain centered her mind, brought her focus. *Get out of here. Get home.* Then, she could fall apart. Yell. Scream. Make effigies of her bosses and poke pins in them.

Bastards.

Forty-three wasn't past it.

She thrust open the doors into the carpark and stomped over to her zippy red coupe. Five minutes later, she peeled from her space and headed home.

She'd do the job at Middlemarch, give her best efforts as she usually did, but it was clear she'd need to come up with a Plan B because Plan A sucked big time.

"They've replaced me on the new show." She glared at her computer screen and the familiar face of Janet, her United States agent. "They're shunting me sideways."

Janet's brows scrunched. "Why?"

"I'm too old."

"They can't do that."

"They've done it," Megan said, fury punching out her words in staccato beats.

"You should write full-time. Your sales are stellar, and the publisher will snap up more from you in a heartbeat. Start that new paranormal romance series you mentioned last year."

"I don't know. Writing is fun, something to fill the long plane flights and the nights in hotel rooms. If I go full-time, I'd worry about the writing becoming a drag. A chore. I love working with the sports team, traveling to commentate games and interview the players. I feel...I feel as though they've spare-tackled me—driven my head into the ground and left me unconscious, away in *la-la* land. The writing is fun, and the fact I've sold and made a decent living is a side benefit. It's something just for me, you know?"

"So what are you going to do?"

Megan sighed, the expulsion of air leaving her lightheaded. She inhaled again while her mind sorted through her alternatives. Her shoulders slumped. "While I don't agree with their ageism, hitting my forties limits my options. I guess I'll do lists of pros and cons and work out what I do want. I have a job in the South Island for this weekend and then a weeklong holiday. Hopefully, I'll come up with Plan B before I have to return to the office. I don't think Jeremy knows what to do with me either."

"You could always self-publish your new series and work at your own pace or take a penname and try something different."

"What? You'd lose out on your fee." Megan smiled at her agent of five years and the woman who had become a friend as well as her tough negotiator and secret weapon.

Janet grinned back. "No, I wouldn't, because my next suggestion is to use our in-house publishing. Win-win for me."

"I'll think about it. Add the idea to my lists." Hadn't she always yearned to write a historical romance? Maybe this was the opportunity to take this step.

"Have you considered writing an autobiography for someone else?"

"Ghost writing?"

"Yes. The agency gets requests from celebrities who can't or won't for whatever reason do their own writing."

"You think I could do that?"

"I do. You're used to interviewing sporting celebrities, asking the hard questions. You've won awards for it. Add the option to your mega lists."

"Are you making fun of my lists?"

"Always," Janet said, the twinkle in her brown eyes removing any sting.

Megan nodded. "Will do. I'd better pack for my trip to this one-horse town. Jeremy didn't give me much notice, even though they received the invitation months ago. He must have intended to send one of the junior commentators, so on top of this, I'll have another employee grousing about me and glaring holes in my back, full of resentment at losing a gig."

"Not your fault," Janet said. "You can't control stuff like this."

"True, but it doesn't make me feel any better."

"Don't worry, sweetie. Look at this as an opportunity."

"Yeah," Megan mumbled, bitterness leaving her empty and exhausted. Some opportunity.

"One more suggestion to add to your list," Janet said, that twinkle appearing in her eyes again.

"What?"

"Find a younger man and let him screw your brains out. That always perks me up."

"Lord, I can't remember when I last...oh, yeah." She brightened then winced. "The last guy I dated was a doctor. He used to break dates because of work commitments. I thought I'd surprise him with dinner one night because he said he had work and needed to cancel our date. I found him screwing his wife. Since then, I've been wary. I have other bad dating stories I haven't told you about yet." *No one even came close to comparing to Charlie.*

"Oh, sweetie." Janet shook her head. "Find a young stud. You're attractive. You won't have any difficulty in finding a man."

"Can I quote you on that?" The job she loved impeded romance, and she'd chosen to focus on her work much to Tessa, her younger sister's disgust. Looking back now, she saw her mistakes. Maybe Tessa with her snooty asides had been correct. "All right, I'll add it to Plan B, but I'm not making any promises."

"This gig at the one-horse town. Is it rugby related?"

"Yes."

Janet waggled her eyebrows. "Then, you have a pool of potential young studs."

"I'm the commentator. I can't sleep with one of the players."

"Why not?"

"I-I..." Her brain stopped working. She had nothing because it was a weekend tournament, and she wasn't responsible for refereeing decisions. There was no conflict of interest if she decided to allow a player to pick her up. Of course, she didn't want a coach bawling her out because she'd exhausted one of his players. Gossip, too, was another consideration. She'd never placed herself in a position where people discussed her morals and didn't intend to start on this path to loss of her reputation. She drew herself up and nodded at the computer screen. "I'll consider the idea."

"That's my girl. And on that note, I'll leave you. Is your latest book coming along nicely? Do we need to shift any deadlines?"

"I sent the final edits into Carol last week, and I've started work on the last book in the trilogy. It's going well. My deadline will be fine since I'll get writing time in while I'm on holiday."

"You're not staying at home?"

"No, depending on the weather, I might zap across to Sydney or drive to Taupo." Charlie, her fiancé, was buried in Taupo, and she hadn't visited for a while.

"Good," Janet said. "I expect a postcard. Go and do some work. Think about your next proposal while you're away. I'm not kidding. Your publisher is keen to sign you for another series."

"I'll do that, Janet. Thanks." Megan hit disconnect and stared at her screen for an instant. A picture of her and Charlie with a background of the Sydney harbor in Australia. They'd just become engaged, their young and innocent faces full of joy. Charlie had proposed to her before he left to join his army squad in Afghanistan. The roadside bomb had changed everything. She sighed and turned off her computer. She should change the picture, but every time she went to do that, something stopped her. They would've celebrated twenty years of marriage now, probably with children...

Megan pushed away from her desk, no longer in the mood to write. She wandered through her harborside apartment, pausing to stare out the window at the dark waters and the lights from the CBD, the harbor bridge and the businesses and homes on the North Shore of the city. She'd always loved her apartment and its central location. Tonight, it felt lonely. Sad.

She grabbed her red coat, a beanie to pull over her blonde hair and her black handbag. She'd go to the nearby hotel for a drink. No, maybe a cocktail. If she found someone to talk to—good. If not, she'd start on her lists. She'd pack once she arrived home. It wouldn't matter if she was late because she'd never sleep tonight, anyway. A snort erupted. Not for the reason Janet might suspect. Anger and frustration still simmered every time she thought of the way they were shuffling her sideways.

Time for Plan B.

CHAPTER TWO

JACOB ANDERSON, KNOWN AS Jacey by his stepson and friends, tore across the brow of the hill in his wolf form. Henry, his stepson, and Leo Mitchell, a leopard shifter and new acquaintance, raced behind him. Geoffrey, Henry's Jack Russell, followed in the rear, his joyous bark filling the air.

Jacey dodged a pile of schist and sped into the coolness of a stand of pine. The wind ruffled his fur. The scent of pine and earth filled every breath along with satisfaction. He'd missed Henry and his friend Gerard. In his heart, Gerard was a second son, and he'd enjoyed seeing the boy marry in the human way in Fiji.

Jacey huffed, his sharp teeth showing in a wolfish smile. London was perfect for Gerard, although a part of him wished he'd met Jenny, the woman Henry had thought his mate. His son had taken the woman's death hard, and Jacey ached for him. He knew the pain of losing a mate.

Leo let out a feline bark, a command to stop and shift. Since he was a newcomer to Middlemarch and Henry hadn't run in this area of the country before, Leo had come along to show them where they could shift in safety.

Jacey pictured his human form and shifted. His breathing came faster than normal, and his skin tingled with the winter chill. Invigorating. He hadn't felt so alive for ages. This move from Australia to New Zealand...he'd come because Henry needed him, but already he liked the town and the people—both shifters and humans—he'd met. Maybe a change was all he needed to cure the intense loneliness assailing him.

"Geoffrey needs to keep quiet in this next spot," Leo warned. "It's safe to run, but the sound might carry to the guests at the farm cottages and attract attention. They can't see this paddock and hill from their cottages but Saber said silence is best to keep curiosity at bay."

Jacey nodded, and Henry stooped to pat his terrier. A series of growls broke out as Henry communicated with his dog. Jacey shook his head, absently noting he needed a haircut. The pair looked incongruous together—the big silent man and the small white-and-black dog, yet Jacey was pleased the boy had the pet to look after. The changes in his son worried him, and he was glad he'd agreed to move to Middlemarch. With the recession in Australia, business was sluggish. He wasn't the only person returning to New Zealand to live. Many families wanted a better life for their children. He shook his head and brushed away an errant strand. He wasn't much different in that respect. Henry mightn't be his son by blood, but the boy owned his heart.

15

He missed Henry and Gerard, and it wasn't as if he had any family left in Perth. Perth had become a habit, a way to keep the memories of his wife alive even though she'd passed when Henry was twelve. It wasn't healthy to live in the past, so he'd agreed to join the boys in their new security business.

Most of the locals had made him welcome, particularly the Mitchell family. His son had told him they were good men, and so far, his instincts steered him in the same direction. There were a few of the feline population who turned their backs on him. Henry had warned him of this, but it still rankled. The time for wolf-feline wars had passed during the nineteenth century, long before his birth. This was the twenty-first century and inter-species wars had no place unless they wanted humans to learn of their existence.

"It's a decent acreage of land in which to run," Jacey said.

"The only thing you can't do around here is vocalize," Henry said. "If we want to do that, we must head to the back country near Mt Cook or Tekapo."

Leo nodded. "Yeah. Saber and the council understand your need to vocalize, but you can't do it here. Oh, except for Halloween, but Saber said he and the council will discuss that with you soon. They're having a town function with a haunted house, and Emily suggested wolf song might work nicely to give anyone a scare."

Jacey glanced at Henry, surprised to see a slight quirk of his lips before it faded. His own mood lightened with relief. Perhaps the old lighthearted Henry still lurked near the surface.

Leo indicated the hillside in front of them with a gesture. "We can run down there, through the manuka trees and that clearing, jump the fence that runs along the ridge and we'll be on Mitchell land. Who is up for a race?" He shifted and took off without giving them a chance to reply.

Jacey and Henry exchanged another glance. Geoffrey growled and trotted a few steps in the direction in which Leo had departed.

"We can't let Pretty Boy beat us," Henry said, and seconds later, they'd shifted and hurtled through the tangle of undergrowth.

Joy spread through Jacey. He lengthened his strides, edging ahead of Henry and gradually reducing Leo's head start. *Huh! Not so old*. Life in the old wolf yet.

The urge to vocalize pounded through his brain in a siren song. Jacey ignored it and kept hurtling toward the trees. He burst from the sunshine into the shadowed trees. Stock traversing the paddock had made a narrow path through the patch of bush, and Jacey charged along the trail, not breaking his pace.

Ahead of him, Leo raced into the clearing. Jacey stormed after him, momentarily blinded by the brighter light. Henry pulled up beside Jacey until they raced neck and neck. Jacey dragged in much needed oxygen. Instead of crisp Otago air, the greenery and soil, he caught a hint of exotic flowers. He slowed, gave a warning bark.

Henry pulled up, and Leo skidded to a halt.

Jacey dragged the air in, working through the layers of scent. Green. Grass. Soil. Tea tree oil from the manuka. Water. Country. All smells he expected. Orange blossom and cinnamon. Chocolate. Those he didn't expect.

He took a halting two steps forward, something in him wanting to follow the foreign scents. They filled him with sudden yearning and hope, an emotion he hadn't embraced since Moira died.

Another step and he saw her, along with the camera phone pointing in their direction.

Jacey dropped to his belly, a sharp rumbly growl warning Henry and Leo to do the same. Geoffrey ran past, his attention on a flitting bird. Joy filled his high-pitched bark as he darted after the thrush.

Jacey continued to watch the woman. Bundled up against the cold in a partially buttoned blue coat with what looked like a black vest beneath, a hat and scarf, she sat on her own beneath a tree, a white pad of some sort keeping her backside dry. Hard to see her expression, but something about her posture screamed isolation and sadness. She snapped a couple more photos before setting down her phone and pulling out a chocolate bar. Although several hundred meters separated them, the crackle of foil carried on the air.

Her gaze tracked Geoffrey's progress across the clearing as she chewed a mouthful of chocolate. Had she not seen them? Her behavior didn't indicate she'd sighted two wolves and a leopard tearing across the country vista in front of her. Fascinated and yet dreading what this might mean, Jacey continued to stare.

The rumblings from a few of the feline population would increase to a roar if they learned he'd put their lives in danger due to his craving for a run and carelessness. No, not quite true. None of them had acted with lack of care, not that their detractors would see it the same way.

Leo crawled up beside him, his feline expression unhappy. Not surprising. They were out in the open and abrupt movement on their part might attract attention.

The woman turned to the panoramic scene on her left and clicked another photo of the sheep-studded paddock on the neighboring farm, the valley and river in the distance, then she aimed the camera at Geoffrey as he bounced through the patches of grass and leaped over rocks.

Time to move.

He slinked across the ground to the nearest cover, a pile of schist rock. Henry and Leo followed without hesitation. The three shifted and stared at each other in consternation.

"I don't know where she came from," Leo said. "There is never anyone here. She must have come from Gilcrest Station. They have cottages for hire, but this is a decent walk from the cottages. Most of the guests come for the fishing or for privacy. They don't wander through the bush and climb fences into private land."

Henry folded his arms across his broad chest. "This one did."

"She didn't react to our presence," Leo said. "I don't know how, but I don't think she saw us. She noticed Geoffrey, but only because he chased the bird."

"He saved us," Jacey said.

"Maybe," Henry offered. "She still has photos. You saw her. She snapped the photos on automatic, but she didn't notice them. If she looks at her snaps later and realizes what she has, we'll be in trouble."

"You're right," Leo agreed in a grim voice. "We must get that phone and delete the photos."

Despite the dire trouble they'd landed themselves in, Jacey grinned. "How the devil are we going to do that?" He gestured at his body with an elegant hand. "I don't think she'd appreciate three naked men approaching her."

"Might cause a problem," Henry said without cracking a grin.

Jacey's heart ached for his son, knowing he'd be experiencing the same gut-wrenching loneliness he felt each day. He could tell Henry the isolation eased, but it didn't go away either. Jacey's nostrils flared as he dragged in a deep breath. The exotic orange blossom and cinnamon filled his senses again. The rich, dark chocolate. He'd bet she was eating a bar of the new chocolate produced by the local manufacturer. No, he wouldn't mention the sense of isolation to Henry.

Jacey turned to Leo. "Do you recognize her?"

"I've never seen her before."

"So what do we do?" Henry asked.

"We follow her," Leo said.

"I'll follow her," Jacey volunteered. "You said that the logical place for her to stay is in the holiday cottages. Why don't you two go back to the vehicle and bring my clothes?"

Leo gave a decisive nod. "If she glimpses you, she's more likely to assume she saw a dog. If she sees me, Saber and the Feline council will get pissed because a sighting might spark rumors of black cats again."

"You'll pick me up near the holiday cottages?"

"Yes," Leo confirmed.

"See you there? Henry, you're taking Geoffrey?"

"Yeah. I'll whistle for him once you're closer to her."

"Plan," Jacey said, and seconds later, he sneaked from behind the schist in his wolf form, every sense focused on the orange-blossom woman. Behind him, Henry summoned Geoffrey, had a whispered exchange with Leo before the pair, too, shifted to animal.

Jacey used the available cover, a few longer clumps of grass and smaller schist rocks, to creep closer to the woman. The scent wafting from her filled his senses, filled his thoughts with unexpected ideas of seduction. He wanted a clearer view of her face.

She scanned the panoramic view in front of her, her gaze flitting over him. Jacey dropped and froze in position, praying she hadn't glimpsed the paleness of his belly and chest. As a youngster, his fur had been a glossy black. These days, a fair amount of white decorated his belly and chest. In his human form, his hair and stubble when he didn't shave was silver.

His heart pounded, a fraction faster than normal, and he frowned as he absorbed the information. Strange. Something in this human woman pulled at his senses and drew him. Part of the reason he'd volunteered for this job. Curiosity and the urge to regain his balance.

The woman stood and shoved the white pad—a plastic bag—into a pocket. Her coat and winter gear still hid her identity and shape, giving him peekaboo glances of her profile and flashes of blonde hair, but her scent...

Jacey breathed deeply, his wolf and his human part wallowing in orange blossom. Now that less distance separated them, there was an underlying earthiness to her aroma. A familiar wolfish scent. No. That made little sense. Another wolf would have scented them, become aware and likely bristled at their intrusion into her solitary state.

No, the woman was human.

This imaginary mystery scent was a puzzle to fill his mind with business. He liked puzzles.

She walked with her shoulders hunched, her head bowed. She sniffed and dragged a hankie from her pocket.

He couldn't see what she was doing, but seconds later, she thrust the hankie back into her pocket and hurried along a narrow path that wound through a stand of native bush. Or at least, Henry had told him the trees were native to New Zealand. Their pungent scent made him want to sneeze.

The path turned, and he glimpsed her face as he followed. She swiped the back of her hand over her eyes with an impatient sigh, knuckling away moisture.

The woman was crying. Ah. That accounted for her absently snapping photos. Her mind lay elsewhere, treading in misery.

Sympathy engulfed Jacey. Empathy. He'd wanted to cry for Henry's loss, for his son's obvious pain. Without a second thought, he let out a doglike whine.

The woman's head snapped up, her shoulders tense, even beneath the heavy jacket. She whirled around, and he glimpsed her blotchy face. The woman was older than his first guess, possibly ten or fifteen years younger than him. Blue eyes like his. Blue eyes swamped with unhappiness.

He whined again, trying to making himself smaller and more doglike. A handy skill. He wagged his tail, wriggled his body. Without taking his gaze off her, he inched closer and tried not to scare her.

"Hey, boy." Her soft voice caressed, even though it held a layer of tears. "Do you belong to the farm or are you lost too?"

Lost? She hadn't acted as if she were lost. Unless she meant Geoffrey? No matter. Jacey approached her with more confidence and lashed his tongue across the back of her hand before she could move. The quick taste of her skin jolted him to the core. Now that he was closer, her scent with that underlying wolf became more obvious, a mystery he wanted to solve. He licked her hand again, his heart racing with unease, with happiness, with fear.

She laughed, still full of tears, but an improvement.

He sidled even closer, leaning his weight against her legs in a silent invitation for petting. Just as well Henry couldn't see him. His son would tease his old man. No, scratch that. Maybe he'd confess to Henry to trigger some teasing. An advance on the son who hardly ever smiled and spent his day immersed in unhappy memories. Jacey wriggled against the woman's hand in encouragement and she ran her hand down his spine.

Every cell in his body stood to attention while his mind did exactly what he'd accused his son of doing—trotted right along memory lane to the moment he'd met Moira.

He'd experienced a similar reaction, although they'd both been in wolf form. It had been a jolt to his senses, and he'd known he could have something special if he pursued the woman.

So, he'd pursued and hadn't regretted his actions for a second. He'd loved Moira and her young son, Henry. The son charming him as much as his mother. He missed Moira every day, and for a time, he'd thought he'd never make it through the pain and yearning for his mate. He'd done it for Henry. As the days passed, he'd mourned and healed. *Mostly*. A part of his life had gone, and he missed Moira, but he'd had Henry to raise on his own. Sure, there had been women over the years, and he'd enjoyed the company and the sex.

With this woman came possibilities, if he decided to explore the simmering attraction flaring to life in him. Dizzy with considering those possibilities, he licked her hand again. Intoxicating. Magical. Crap, he was turning sappy. His son truly would laugh.

Humor flashed through Jacey. And again, he'd consider confessing to Henry because it'd be worth hearing Henry's cackle. But first...

If he followed her back to her cabin, he might gain entry in his wolf form. Then, all he'd need to do was wait until she slept, shift, grab the phone and hit delete, then shift back to wolf. Yeah, that might work. No muss. No fuss.

"Do you belong to the farm, fella? Come on. We should both get back to the warmth. Not only is Middlemarch in the back of beyond, but it's cold too." She scratched him behind the ears, patted him on the head and set off down a path winding between the trees.

Totally the wrong direction.

Jacey sighed. She was pretty with her blonde hair and blue eyes, the faint dusting of freckles across the bridge of her nose giving her a youthful appearance. Her shape was pleasing—what he could see of her beneath the coat. A bad sense of direction wasn't a great flaw.

He pushed past her and stopped in the middle of the track. He whined and gently shunted her back a step.

"Hey!"

Her voice thrilled him. Rich and throaty, a familiarity tugged at him, yet he was certain they'd never met. He never forgot a scent.

Jerking himself from the sensual trap her voice had spun, he whined and pushed past her again. With a sharp bark, he attempted to tell her she was walking the wrong way.

She stared at him with those big blue eyes. "Are you sure?"

Intelligent. He liked that in a woman. Jacey barked again and led the way, making sure to wag his tail. He had a sexy arse, according to his past lovers. Moira had assured him that even in wolf form that remained true. He heard the echo of Moira's laughter, tinkling and happy, and he smiled inside, wagging his tail faster.

Just before she'd passed, Moira had made him promise to find someone else to love when the time was right. His memory trotted out the painful scene. He'd promised, of course, but he hadn't meant the words.

It's time, Jacob. Henry has grown into a fine adult. It's time for you now.

Startled by the thought that sounded like Moira speaking to him, he halted. The woman walked into him, tripped somehow. She let out a squeak and scrabbled for balance, her right hand seizing his tail to help her keep her footing. She yanked, and Jacey let out a startled bark. He jerked from the contact and dashed a few steps ahead.

"Oomph!"

Jacey heard the sound then a grunt. He whirled with a growl, and found her sitting on her butt in the middle of the track, her blue eyes wide at his ill-humored snarl.

"Good doggy," she whispered, her gaze wary, her brows drawn together.

Hell, she thought he intended to bite her. He'd never do that. He eased closer to her, trying to appear smaller and harmless.

"G-good doggy." She didn't take her eyes off him as he approached. "Y-you l-look like a wolf."

Jacey froze, unsure of what to do next. He whimpered and dropped into a submissive position, the leaf-strewn ground cool against his belly. He crawled closer and her fear faded beneath a smile. Her fingers sank into his ruff, and Jacey sighed in pleasure.

"Well," she said finally. "I should go. My butt is frozen."

He backed up, missing the physical contact. He wanted to wallow in her scent and presence. Instead, he watched her clamber to her feet and brush off her butt.

The least he could do was get her walking in the right direction. Jacey trotted along the track and turned to bark at her. He moved a few more steps and barked at her in expectation.

She frowned. "Are you sure? I could have sworn I walked this way earlier."

Jacey barked and wished he could shift and tell the woman she'd end up lost if she insisted on following her sense of direction. She hesitated, and he barked again.

"All right," she said. "But if we end up lost, I will cry. I don't cry pretty. Anyone can see that. I might have already cried over the direction my life has taken, but there are more tears inside me. I can feel them. They're sitting there waiting for the floodgates to open. And I'm talking to a dog. Fine. I'll follow you, but there had better be a hot shower and a big glass of red wine waiting for me."

Jacey gave a wolfish grin and set off weaving between the trees, reassured once he heard her stumbling after him and mumbling under her breath. About men of all things. His grin widened. He looked forward to furthering his acquaintance with this woman, learning her name.

But first, he needed to check out the photos she'd snapped with her smartphone.

CHAPTER THREE

PLAN B. IT WASN'T going too well. She'd spent the morning walking and blubbering, and now she had a wet butt. She could feel the clinging slide of her silky underwear with each step and a chill had sunk to her bones. The path exited the trees, and she glimpsed the farm cottages, one of which she was renting for the week. Apparently, the dog was correct, and she'd been getting herself lost too.

Megan snorted, the sound emerging with an edge of tears and the dog shot her a look, its ears pricking. "What is with you, dog? It's my party, and I'll cry if I want to."

Yes! That was another *look*, complete with rising doggy eyebrows.

It was official. *All* males sucked.

A pity because she enjoyed sex, and her trusty vibrator wasn't always a good substitute.

"Let's go."

She noted the rear end of a SUV parked on the far side of the neighboring cottage. Perhaps her luck would bloom, and she'd find a sexy younger man right next door to build up her confidence. Another snort emerged, this one stronger and angrier. Her gaze zapped to the dog, and she discovered he'd stopped and turned to stare at her with those freaky blue eyes. And his eyebrows rose again in a question.

"Who do you belong to?" She did not want to deal with a lost dog, although this one seemed to know his way about. "The station owner, right?"

He yipped, a sharp, impatient bark.

"Okay. Okay. Shower. Big glass of red wine." Megan stomped down the gentle incline until she reached the sealed parking area. Landscaped gardens full of native flax and miniature hebes, a green hedging plant, these covered with tiny purple flowers, edged the sealed area. Subtle security lamps lit the way at night, giving a magical appearance. If she wasn't so worried about her future, she might have enjoyed her visit to Middlemarch.

The organizers of the Sevens tournament had left a welcome package containing snacks, the bottle of red wine and a floral arrangement that included a note with an invitation for dinner tomorrow night. Emily Mitchell, who wrote the letter, introduced herself and mentioned she'd taken the place of the man who'd contacted the network. He'd passed away suddenly, and Emily hoped her replacing Kenneth Nesbitt was okay. The woman had provided red wine. Okay with Megan.

Megan headed for her stone cottage. The dog waited at

29

her door, as if he expected to enter. His tail wagged, his ears pricked, and those blue eyes held pleading.

"No, you can't come inside. You're wet and muddy."

The dog stepped away from her and shook vigorously. She blinked, felt her mouth drop open as she stared. The dog shook a second time, and Megan frowned. Weird. *Plain weird*.

She pulled her room key from the zipped pocket of her vest and shoved it in the lock. On automatic, she patted the matching pocket on the right side of her vest for her phone. Losing that would put a seal on her crappy day, but no, it was there. She yawned, exhausted from her walk and crying jag. Perhaps she'd take a snooze before the wine. She opened the door, and the dog pushed past before she could stop it.

"Hey! You go back to wherever you came from."

The dog ignored her and settled in front of a wall heater with an expectant glance in her direction. He was doing well with communication. Next, he'd speak to her.

Megan shook her head at her inventive thoughts. Too fanciful. It was no wonder she'd made a second career of writing romance with *her* imagination. Now she was assigning a personality to this dog. The wretched creature had probably pulled this stunt with previous guests.

"Fine," she muttered and stripped off her coat. She dumped it over the back of a chair and stooped to unzip her black boots, then hopped like an ungainly stork while she removed them.

The dog barked—a short yet demanding yip—and glanced at the heater.

"Fine," she snapped again, but a sneaking admiration pushed into her mind. This was one bright dog. "A freaky pair of blue eyes will only get you so far, mister." Megan flipped the wall switch, and the heater clicked and hummed to life.

Megan padded through the open-plan lounge and kitchen area to one of the two luxurious bedrooms. Everything in the cottage spoke of luxury and good taste, a blend of cream and different shades of brown in the furnishings and the local artwork on the walls making the place comfortable and inviting relaxation. The same ambience radiated from the bedroom and attached en suite. A plush cream robe hung on the back of the en suite door. Fluffy cream towels with chocolate-brown accents hung on rails, ready for her use.

In the bedroom, she stripped off her damp clothes, placed her phone by her pillow, and naked, she headed straight to the shower cubicle. She opened the door and flipped on the water mixer. Warm water poured down, and she ducked under the spray. She regulated the temperature and adjusted the controls for a second showerhead. The water pounded her back. A sigh slipped free. Perfect. Just perfect.

Ten minutes later, feeling much warmer and cleaner, she slipped into an oversize T-shirt, closed the blinds to shut out the day and crawled into bed. She picked up her phone, intending to ring her contacts, Saber or Emily Mitchell, but instead closed her eyes and drifted, her exhausted mind craving sleep.

Jacey listened to the shower switch on as he turned to warm his other side. His eyelids slipped shut, and he jerked them open again. *Crap.* He couldn't go to sleep. He needed to get his hands on that phone and delete the photos she'd taken of them. His happiness, Henry's happiness, depended on it, and damned if he'd let the community chase off Henry because of an innocent mistake. Henry had settled here in Middlemarch and didn't need more turmoil in his life.

He shook himself and cast out his senses. The shower was still going. He'd check her coat pocket. Unfortunately, he hadn't seen where she put her phone. She'd slipped it away while he, Henry and Leo had held their strategy meeting. Jacey listened again and heard the shower cease. Bother, he'd thought she might dally. He needed to hurry.

Jacey shifted, shot a quick glance in the direction of the bedroom and headed toward the chair where she'd left her coat. He rifled through the pockets and came up empty. Damn it. Why couldn't this be easy?

Resigned, he stalked toward the bedroom. She was in the en suite. If he was quick and lucky, he might find the phone on the bedside cabinet or out in the open for her to grab if it rang.

At the bedroom doorway, he listened, and when he heard nothing, he peeked around the corner. She was still in the en suite. He'd risk it. At the last second, he stopped and shifted to wolf. While she mightn't be happy to see him wandering around her bedroom in his wolf form, she'd freak if she saw a strange naked man. And if she saw

32

his face, that would put a full stop on him getting to know her better.

Bother the woman. She was a problem on all fronts, a threat to his wolf and to the man.

He shifted, and not a second too soon. The woman strolled into the room wrapped in a towel. She pulled something bright blue from her bag, dropped the towel and pulled on a shapeless T-shirt.

Jacey blinked at the shapely blonde. Slim waist. Curvy hips. Breasts a nice handful and pert for her age. A natural blonde. Before he knew it, cloth screened her nakedness from neck to knee. He focused on the design on the front of the T-shirt. It read *Loch Ness Monster* and had a picture of Nessie with his head showing above the lake waters. He resented that monster, blocking his view. Scowling, he shook himself back to the job at hand. While he'd been staring at the T-shirt and mourning its presence, the woman had drawn the blinds and slid into the bed. She gave a gusty sigh and settled on her side, facing the window.

Perfect for his purposes.

Jacey padded into the bedroom, the woolen carpet soft beneath his paws. He approached the bed. Nothing on the bedside cabinet apart from a notepad and what looked like an e-reader in a purple case. Bathroom next. A floral scent greeted him when he slinked into the en suite and reared up on his hind legs to survey the countertop. The same floral scent he'd registered on her earlier, but stronger. Toiletries graced the countertop—a yellow toothbrush, a tube of toothpaste, a comb and a brush. No phone.

Her clothes lay in a heap on the floor where she'd kicked

them aside. The messiness pleased him since no one liked perfect. Hands would be better suited for this job. With a swift glance at the bed, he shifted and checked her pockets. Nothing again.

Damn, what had she done with the phone?

Jacey returned to wolf. He reared up to check the tallboy dresser on the far side of the bed, but couldn't see the phone. A gruff sound of frustration escaped him and the woman stirred in the bed.

She rolled toward him and rubbed her eyes. "What are you doing in here, doggie? Out! You are not getting in this bed with me."

Jacey froze as his mind wandered in the direction her words sent it. Bed. Woman. Nakedness. His heart raced while every muscle in his body stiffened. Images flashed of bodies writhing against each other. Shock coated some of the visions since he hadn't craved a woman with this intensity for a long time, not since Moira entered his life and changed everything.

"Out," the woman ordered.

Jacey turned and trotted from the bedroom, forcing his limbs to move when every particle of him wanted to approach, shift to human form and slide into the bed next to this sexy woman. Crap, he didn't even know her name. He could fix that soon enough, but finding the phone was more important right now.

Out in the open space of the lounge, he checked all the surfaces, even though he knew she hadn't set the phone down here. Nothing. The only possible place it could be was in the bed with her. A surge of disappointment flooded him. Not a workaholic? He didn't need someone like that in his life. While he worked hard, he liked to play and enjoy himself too. No point working so hard that life flew by without enjoyment.

They'd have to get the phone another time, because although urgency drilled through him, there was no way he was invading her bed or frightening her into giving up the phone. A man had to have standards, and those were his. He never frightened women. Men who used their brute force to control the opposite sex were below contempt. Moira's first husband, for example.

Conceding defeat, Jacey shifted to human and slipped from the cottage. He surveyed his surroundings, saw nothing or no one out of place, and closed the door behind him with a soft click. He darted over to the next cottage where Leo and Henry waited in Henry's SUV.

Leo opened the passenger door and handed out Jacey's jeans. "Any luck?"

"The woman took the phone to bed with her. What kind of person takes a phone to bed with them?" Jacey demanded in frustration.

Henry scowled from the driver's seat. "Hell."

"I was hoping we'd handle this without having to confess to Saber," Leo said, sounding resigned. "Emily mentioned she'd invited the woman to dinner. Scoring Megan Saxon as our commentator is a big deal, and Emily wanted to make sure she enjoys her visit to Middlemarch."

"That's her name? Megan?" Jacey asked.

"Yeah. You haven't heard of her? She does special-interest pieces on rugby players, interviews and commentates some of the games. You mightn't have seen her on the telly in Australia," Leo said. "I thought there was something familiar about her but it took a while to click. Megan Saxon is not the right person to take a photo of us in our animal forms. She will ask questions."

"She's a reporter?" A trace of horror coated Henry's sharp words.

The same dismay rippled through Jacey. His day kept getting worse. "What should we do now?"

Leo scowled. "As I said, we'll have to tell Saber. Isabella is gonna laugh off her butt. The awfulness of my teenage years coming back to haunt me. I hope Saber finds humor in the situation. Felix, my older brother, and I used to go around getting into trouble. The twins too. Saber says we gave him gray hair." He glanced at Jacey, scanned his silver hair and chuckled. "Henry must have been a right handful."

"Not helping," Henry said. "Right, we'll head to Saber's and confess."

Jacey had already met Saber Mitchell and his wife, Emily. He'd liked the younger couple and sensed their happiness. Jacey didn't, however, want to cause trouble for the man. It wasn't too late to toss him and Henry out of the Middlemarch community. Saber and the rest of the feline residents could make things very uncomfortable for them.

Ten minutes later, Henry pulled up in front of the Mitchell residence. "Well, let's face the music."

Lucky for them, Leo Mitchell had been present, otherwise they'd be at an even greater disadvantage.

Jacey and Henry followed Leo up the flower-edged

footpath to the front door. They waited while Leo thumped on the white front door then opened it.

"Saber, you there?" Leo wiped his feet on the doormat and entered.

Emily appeared at the end of a long passage, wiping her hands on an orange towel. Her long jumper stretched over the curve of her pregnant belly. "You've just caught him. He popped in for a cup of tea before heading out to muster the sheep. Who is with you? Oh, Henry. Jacey. Come in and have tea."

They trailed Leo down the passage, catapulting Jacey back to his school days with memories of visiting the school principal. He'd also been a mischievous teenager, not that he'd admit it to these two.

"Hi, how did the run go?" Saber stood and gestured to the empty chairs around the kitchen table.

Jacey shared a glance with Leo and Henry.

"Not so good," Leo said after a long pause. "We were running in the north paddock where we've run before. There was a woman there, sitting under a tree. She snapped a couple of photos. I don't think she saw us, but when she looks at her photos later, she'll realize she snapped more than the scenery."

"Anyone we know," Saber asked, his green eyes alert.

"Megan Saxon," Leo said. "I didn't recognize her right away. Henry and I went back to collect our clothes and the SUV while Jacey went with her, hoping to retrieve her phone so he could delete the pictures."

"It didn't work?" Emily asked.

"She thought I was a dog," Jacey said. "I went with her

back to the cottage at Gilcrest Station and got inside. I searched for her phone while she was in the shower and checked the bedroom. She'd gone to sleep, but I woke her up, and she ordered me from her bedroom. The only place the phone could have been was in the bed with her. I'm sorry. I tried to find it."

"If you were running in the north paddock, you weren't out of order," Saber said. "Leo was with you."

"Try telling that to the militant felines," Emily muttered as she set empty mugs on the kitchen table. She plonked onto an empty chair next to Saber. "Milk?"

"Please," Jacey said.

"Yes, please," Henry said.

Emily poured their tea and shunted mugs in their direction. "Have a chocolate chip cookie. One of you could ask her out for dinner," she suggested.

"Not me," Henry said, his manner emphatic.

"I'm out. Isabella would gut me," Leo said with a grin. "Then she'd do something diabolical to the woman, just to make her point."

Everyone turned to Jacey, their expressions ranging from amusement to determination. Jacey sighed. "I guess we could try that, but how am I going to meet her? I can't bowl up there and ask her out. She doesn't know me. She'll think I'm a stalker, someone interested in her public face. She'll think I want to use her fame for my glory." The last thing Jacey wanted was a woman in his life who was public property. It wasn't too late to walk away. He'd scarcely touched her. A lick didn't count. He took a shallow breath, but it did little to quell the surge of panic

38

bouncing around his stomach like a pinball. A lick—two licks weren't enough to cement a bond. There was no bond. Jacey closed his eyes and forced away the memory of her orange blossom scent and the faint wolfish musk on her skin. "Couldn't we break into the cottage or pretend to be a cleaner?"

He glanced up from his mug of tea and caught Henry's gaze. His son was eyeing him with concern.

"What?" Jacey demanded. "The longer we leave it the more danger we're in. Maybe she didn't get a photo of us, but what if she did? She could have seen the photo already. She could have emailed it to her network or a media contact."

"You're not to scare her," Emily ordered. "She's coming here for dinner tomorrow night. Ah! I have a better idea. I intended to suggest to Saber that we raffle off a dinner date with her. We could swing it so Jacey wins the date. Voila, dinner for two. You'll have to pay for a ticket though. I was thinking ten or twenty dollars for each ticket. Since we're rigging the raffle, you'd have to pay five hundred." She winked at Saber, and he sent her a lazy grin, an intimate one that made Jacey feel like an interloper.

"Emily," Leo protested. "Two things. You can't extract money like that, even for a good cause, and stop matchmaking for Jacey. I'm sure he can get his own dates without your shenanigans."

"We can't delay until tomorrow," Jacey warned, ignoring the dating and matchmaking part of the conversation.

She wagged her finger. "The three of you have made this

problem. Even though it wasn't your fault, it's right you suffer the consequences."

"Saber." Leo turned to his older brother, but Saber smiled and clasped Emily's hand.

"Emily has a point," he said. "Next time you'll remember to scent and scan the vicinity before you charge across a piece of open ground."

"Not helpful," Leo snapped.

"Jacey's right," Saber said, the humor fading from his expression. "We need that phone tonight. Kitten, you can still punish them by making them pay for a date."

"Tsk-tsk. I'm shocked that you and Emily would consider fixing the raffle," Leo commented. "If word got out—"

"Enough," Emily said. "You will pay the extra money as a fine for not double-checking for human presence. Any kitten knows to check and recheck before running through an area in feline form."

Saber chuckled, his affection for his mate clear. "She's got you there."

Jacey sipped his tea, his mind spinning with alternative plans. "I didn't see any food, apart from the gift basket in her room. Won't she have to go out to get food at some stage?" He turned to Emily. "Invite her to meet you at your café for an early dinner. Tell her you need to clarify a few things and they're time sensitive."

"Not bad," Saber said.

"And if she says no?" Emily asked.

"They have a dining room at the station for their guests. If you mention food, she might decide she is hungry." Leo groaned. "Isabella will never let me hear the end of this. Emily, give Ms. Saxon a call and tell her you'd like to run through the plan today rather than tomorrow since you have last-minute hiccups."

"I don't have any hiccups," Emily said, giving him a hard stare.

"Tell her some of your people have come down with the flu, and you wanted to check on how many helpers she requires," Saber suggested.

"An excuse as transparent as a piece of lace," Emily said in a tart tone.

Saber lifted her hand and kissed it. "I'm sure you'll think of something suitable to tell her."

"Women have to swoop in and save the day all the time." Emily freed her hand and grabbed a cookie. "We fix up messes. That's what we do." She bit into the chocolate chip cookie with a snap of her teeth.

Jacey hid a smile.

"We could always enter the cottage, blindfold her and take the phone," Henry said in a mild voice.

Emily bolted upright, her spine hitting the back of the chair. "No."

Jacey didn't think much of the idea either. He'd hate to scare her witless.

"It might come to that." Jacey faced the truth even though he disliked it. "Right, this is the plan. Emily can call her. Please. If she says no to the meeting, we'll meet at the cottage and play it by ear."

Emily nodded, although she remained somber as she stood to pick up a phone. As the phone rang, she turned her back on them.

From where he was sitting, Jacey heard the dial tone and the feminine voice as the woman—Megan—answered the call.

"Hi, Ms. Saxon. This is Emily Mitchell. I'm very sorry to bother you but I wondered if we could have our meeting this evening, perhaps during an evening meal? Something has come up, and I need to change our plans slightly."

Emily paused, and Jacey strained to hear Megan's reply.

"Oh, I'm sorry to hear that. I hope it's nothing serious."

Megan spoke again. Jacey couldn't make out the words, just the tone. His orange-blossom girl sounded depressed. Had she been crying again?

"Tomorrow morning? That would be perfect," Emily said. "I own the Storm in a Teacup café. Could you meet me there at ten? Great. I'm looking forward to meeting you in person. Yes, I'll see you there." Emily hung up and turned to face them. "I tried. She said she'd had a long, difficult week and was having an early night as soon as she'd eaten dinner. You should go now in case you can nip in and grab the phone."

"Isabella is expecting me," Leo said.

"Don't sweat it," Henry said. "Jacey and I will take care of it."

Jacey set down his mug and stood. "Let's go."

Henry joined him before continuing the conversation. "She might already have someone."

"Was she wearing a ring?"

Not a single piece of jewelry on her hands. "No, but that means nothing."

"Really? This is not the cheerful, enthusiastic and positive father of my childhood."

"It feels...weird. As if I'm being unfaithful to Moira." The truth, as far as it went, but Megan drew his interest, his curiosity.

"Opportunities like this don't come along often," Henry said, his brown gaze full of stormy passion and challenge. "I'd be disappointed in you, disappointed in myself, if I didn't urge you to at least see if she might be the one for you. You'll regret it every day if you let her walk away without at least trying."

"Do you think she's friends with a wolf? Or has a boyfriend? Husband?" Jacey wasn't normally this indecisive, but Megan Saxon's scent got to him, raised nerves. Anticipation and a healthy dose of anxiety. What if he was making a mistake?

"The wolf scent isn't strong. Could be transference. If she had a mate, the scent would be stronger."

Jacey tapped his fingers on the dash while he eyed the dining room. Did he want to pursue her? His inner wolf whined, loud enough for Henry to hear.

His son shifted his weight. "I think your wolf has already made your decision for you."

MEGAN PICKED UP HER glass and sipped the red wine. Hints of berry and pepper teased her palate before she swallowed. She'd had misgivings about the family-style dining but it turned out dinner was a table of one tonight, which was fine since she didn't feel like company.

A fire crackled in the hearth while she sat at a table far enough away not to get overheated and close enough to take the chill from her bones. Subdued lighting glinted off crystal glasses and silverware. A vase containing a single pink carnation and a piece of lacy fern graced her table. Real, she discovered on fingering the greenery. She rifled through her coat, slung over the second chair at her table, to retrieve her phone, the only thing she'd brought from the cottage. She switched it on, but didn't bother checking her text messages. Tomorrow was soon enough, but habit had her placing it within reach, in case her younger sister or her brother-in-law called.

A swift pang of envy struck, pushed away with a sharp kick of her mind. Tessa had told her she'd regret choosing her career over having children. No! Jealousy had no place in her life, and not for a sister who sniped at her about her decisions. Tessa didn't understand that after Charlie, work was all she'd had.

A thin and dark-haired waitress arrived with a bowl of fragrant tomato soup dotted with herb croutons. "Enjoy," she said with a pleasant smile.

"Thanks," Megan said, her stomach rumbling. "It smells great."

"It's a set menu tonight. Would you like the venison or the salmon for your main course? Or we have a vegetarian option."

"The venison please." She'd been craving red meat—another thing Tessa disapproved of since too much meat wasn't healthy.

"Good choice. It's my favorite. The chef prepares the gravy with berries, and it makes the dish," the waitress said and bustled toward the kitchen.

Megan took her time with her meal, the good food relaxing her, the tension seeping from her shoulders. *Plan B*. She lifted her glass of wine in a toast. Yup, she was gonna do it. She could scope out the locals tomorrow when she went to meet Emily Mitchell at the café. Janet's idea of finding a younger lover looked better and better the more she considered the different angles.

Since it was a rugby tournament, she shouldn't have any trouble finding a man to fit her specifications.

It was almost two hours later when she stood, pulled on her coat and slipped her phone into her coat pocket. She bid farewell to the still smiling waitress and wandered outside to return to her cottage.

It was cooler outside, and she staggered, feeling the effects of the bottle of wine.

Oops. She listed to the right, over-corrected and lurched to the left. *Oopsie.* She giggled and concentrated on putting one foot in front of the other. "Not much farther," she muttered. "Just got to get to the cottage."

At least she shouldn't have problems sleeping tonight. A good thing. "Too much time wasted on worrying 'bout the future."

As she neared her cottage, two men appeared in front of

her. She halted abruptly, blinked. Whoa! Nice specimens. She blinked again because her vision had turned fuzzy, and she hated to miss this spectacle.

"Hello." Her voice emerged in a husky breath, and she tipped back her head to stare up at them. No heels for her tonight. She wasn't a shrimp, but these two men stood inches above her five foot eight.

"Hi." The younger one had light brown hair or it might have been dark blond. Difficult to tell in this light. It was long and with his beefy build, he reminded her of the hero of her most recent release. He studied her, and she thought she saw a flicker of interest. Her pulse jumped into a rapid *cha-cha-cha*. Maybe she wouldn't need to wait until tomorrow. Tall and sexy had strolled right up to her cottage.

The older one smiled, and she thought she saw evidence of crinkles at the corners of his eyes, but she wasn't sure if her mind played her. Moving on. His gray hair was cut short. He moved closer. Light-colored eyes. Blue perhaps? Attractive in an older-man way. One or both of them wore a lovely aftershave. It tempted her to sidle closer. It whispered of sin.

She turned her attention back to younger Tall and Sexy. An audition. Yeah. No point pursuing a dud. She took a stumbling step toward Tall and Sexy. The man didn't smile, but she could fix that. She was good at fixing stuff. 'Sides, she didn't need him to smile between the sheets. All she needed was a man who understood directions and didn't mind following them. Younger men liked to learn things. She knew a thing or two, had amassed knowledge over the years. Yeah, teacher role would work as long as he was an apt pupil.

Megan took another step toward the younger man and tripped. His hands shot out to grasp her hips, and she giggled. So far, so good.

"T-thank you," she said and beamed up at him as her fingers absorbed the hard plane of chest muscles. *Nice*. Time for that kiss.

She moved her hands and linked them behind his neck, stretching at the same time, her gaze on his sensual lips. Her aim was perfect. She knew it was, but at the last instant, he turned his head and her kiss ended up on a lean, bristly cheek. Drat. Tall and Sexy smelled good though.

A growl came from behind them, and she stiffened. Was it that dog again? He seemed to turn up and disappear at will. Tall and Sexy tensed too. His hands moved to hers and tugged them down. It was a polite brush-off, but a brush-off nonetheless. She stepped back, listed, and Tall and Sexy's hands shot out to aid her balance. He caressed her back and hip, waited until she stood under her own steam and only then did he step away.

"Are you all right, ma'am?"

Heat blistered her cheeks at his polite inquiry. Oh boy. She'd done it now. Made an unwanted advance. "S-sorry." She didn't attempt to hold his gaze, her own shooting south to stare at her favorite pair of black boots. Drinking an entire bottle of red wine hadn't been her brightest idea.

"Are you staying at one of the other cottages?" a rich voice asked.

The older man, she presumed. "Yes." She couldn't look

at either man.

"We haven't been here long," Tall and Sexy said. "Wanted to stretch our legs before we retired for the night."

Oh. *Oh!* Were they...

"Which cottage?" the older man asked. "My son and I will escort you home."

"N-no. I'm fine. Don't have far to walk." She willed steel to her traitorous limbs and took a jerky step toward her cottage. *One foot after the other. She could do this. She would do this.*

Two minutes later, she arrived at her door. A security light switched on, almost blinding her.

"Let me." Tall and Sexy's arm reached past her to open her front door.

Megan frowned. She was sure she'd locked her door. Maybe not. She'd left in a hurry because she'd been running late for her dinnertime. Besides, it was so quiet here.

She turned to face the two men and swallowed. They were both gorgeous specimens. Father and son. They didn't bear similar features, but they both stared back at her unblinking and with a military air. Neither smiled this time, their stern features bringing another rush of heat to her cheeks. She, who never blushed or became flustered, had blushed twice in five minutes.

"Thank you," she said, suddenly very sober and aware of her shortcomings. She turned away and stepped over the cottage threshold, sucking in a quick breath. She forced herself to turn and face their stern faces again. "Good night."

She shut the door and wished she could wipe away her shameless actions of the last ten minutes as easily. If she met Tall and Sexy again during the weekend, she'd repeat her apology. Hopefully, he wouldn't make a big deal of her drunken state and tell the press. As a public figure, she needed to take care with her reputation. A sobering reminder. She couldn't let this setback derail her. While she could and would move ahead with Plan B, she'd refrain from drinking and choose wisely.

Plan B was about liberation. Self-destruction wasn't part of the equation.

"I GOT THE PHONE," Henry said.

"Good." Jacey struggled to bat his wolf into submission. His wolf pushed against his skin, pushed, pushed, *pushed* for freedom. A growl squeezed past his teeth, rushing up from his belly. He lengthened his steps in a hurry to get to Henry's vehicle. Henry wasn't interested in the woman, but it hurt that the first female who caught his attention made a pass at his son. He didn't doubt if Henry had shown interest, Megan Saxon would have dragged his son into her bed.

Another growl escaped him, sharp enough to burn his throat as it roared free.

"Stop," Henry snapped, striding to keep up.

But Jacey wasn't in control, knew it, admitted it, even though none of this was Henry's fault. A part of him, the part his wolf wasn't controlling, groped for the shreds of restraint. He dragged in a breath. A second. A third.

He was aware of Henry waiting at his side, giving him space, yet standing his ground. Jacey shoved at his wolf and silently demanded him to settle. Henry didn't want the woman. *Do you hear? Henry isn't interested in Megan Saxon.*

Jacey forced himself to march around the front of the SUV. He opened the passenger door and climbed inside. As soon as they arrived home, he'd go for a short, fast run around Henry and Gerard's property. Rid himself of this tension. If Megan Saxon wasn't interested in him, he'd keep away from temptation.

Simple.

Henry opened the driver's door. "Is it safe for me to get in?"

"Of course. I would never hurt you. You're my son."

"You wanted to bite me a few minutes ago."

"My wolf is under control," Jacey said, and this time he sounded testy.

Henry barked out a harsh snicker and slid behind the wheel. He thumbed the phone to life.

"Password protected?"

"No." Henry clicked on several icons. "She snapped a photo of us." Henry showed it to him.

Jacey grunted. While he and Henry might be mistaken for large dogs at a quick glance, Leo looked like the leopard he was—an animal that shouldn't be running through a New Zealand paddock.

Henry deleted two photos, then removed the photos

and the opening match of the tournament to take place under lights during the evening. Originally, she was meant to meet Emily Mitchell, who represented the council, at a pre-match dinner, but this earlier meeting meant she could plan the way she handled the evening instead of ad-libbing. She could also ask the woman about the town to get an idea of where to focus her special-interest piece. Something to do with the Sevens rugby tournament, for sure.

She nodded her thanks to the waitress who delivered her cup of coffee and a fresh-from-the-oven blueberry muffin. "I'm meant to be meeting Emily Mitchell," she said to the teenage waitress. "I'm early, so tell her not to worry if she's not ready to see me yet. I have planning to do."

"Emily should arrive soon." The teenager's black ponytail swished. "She said she had a meeting. I'll let her know you're here."

"Thank you." Megan picked up her latte and took her first sip, almost moaning at the surge of caffeine. Strong and hot. Most places made wishy-washy coffee. This stuff...excellent. Megan drank a second hit and glanced at her phone when it buzzed with an incoming text.

She'd mislaid her phone during her drunken antics the previous night. To her relief, she discovered it had dropped from her coat pocket at her front door and was none the worse for wear.

The text was from her sister. *Still big & fat with my future rugby player on board! How are the boonies? XX*

Quiet & pretty. Excellent coffee, she typed.

She flicked through her photos, intending to send one and frowned. Only one photo there? She was sure she'd

57

taken more of the countryside with the weird piles of rock. Must have been more out of it yesterday than she thought. Probably the reason for her ill-fated pick-up attempt. Disappointment had made commonsense leak from her brain. Besides... Her fingers pressed into the sides of her coffee cup a little harder. Just because she and Janet thought a younger man would work for her purposes, it didn't mean the young man she propositioned had to go along with the plan. The one last night certainly hadn't. She hadn't seen the men this morning, or maybe she'd misunderstood, because the nearest cottage had appeared empty.

Even now, embarrassed heat flooded her cheeks. *Don't dwell, stupid.* Move on and don't make the same mistake again. Megan attached the one photo she had—thankfully, in focus—and hit send on her text.

Her phone peeped again. *What about men?*

Megan pulled a face. Her younger sister never stopped her matchmaking, positive that Megan would die alone. *Too soon to tell & too busy. Work.*

When her phone remained silent, she focused on her coffee, her blueberry muffin and her surroundings. The café did a brisk trade with people of all ages coming in for coffee and food.

A woman—obviously pregnant—approached her table, a broad smile in place. Her layered brown hair glinted with golden highlights in the sun coming through the front window of the café. She held out her hand in greeting. "Emily Mitchell. Sorry I'm a little late."

Megan stood and shook hands. "Megan Saxon. No

problem. I've been enjoying sitting here in the sunshine coming through the window. You have excellent coffee. The muffins aren't bad either."

The doorbell tinkled, and Emily glanced over. She muttered under her breath, her smile not shifting.

Megan thought she heard a damn and a blast, and something about inconsiderate bus drivers.

"I apologize," Emily said. "I'll need to help my staff deal with this influx of customers. I would read the tour operator the riot act about not giving us pre-warning, but the business helps. Is that a latte? I'll send you over another one. I have another helper starting at ten thirty, so I shouldn't be long."

"It's fine. I wanted to write up notes for a special-interest piece. Happy to wait for you." Normally a fluid starting time for an appointment would drive Megan crazy, but she could see Emily Mitchell was telling the truth and for once, she was glad to sit and relax. The opportunities for downtime didn't come along often.

EMILY HURRIED AWAY FROM Megan Saxon. Rachel, the girl on the counter, was quick and efficient. It was the kitchen where her presence would work best.

"Bus load of tourists has arrived," she said briskly as she grabbed a white chef's coat to cover her clothes. "I'll be with you in a sec. I need to make a quick phone call." She lifted the mobile handset of the landline. "Need anything from the freezer?"

"Butter to soften. Golden syrup and treacle from the pantry."

"Done," Emily said and took the phone with her. In the storeroom, she dialed Henry and Gerard's number and prayed Henry answered rather than Jacey.

"A and D Security," Henry's familiar voice answered.

"Oh good. You're there. Are Gerard and London back from their honeymoon today?" she asked, not bothering to state her name since Henry would recognize her voice.

"Yes." Henry was a man of few words.

"I got the impression your father was interested in meeting Megan Saxon. She is here at the café right now for a meeting with me. I've had a busload of customers turn up and she's willing to wait. Now would be a perfect time for Jacey to come to the café to pick up some of London's favorite chocolate brownies as a welcome home gift."

"I see."

There was a long pause, and Emily wondered if she'd misjudged the situation.

"Dad likes chocolate brownies. I'm off to pick up Gerard and London." He hung up.

Emily pulled a face at the phone. Sometimes, a person needed a few more words to communicate a plan or their acceptance of said plan.

CHAPTER FIVE

JACEY CLIMBED OUT OF Henry's SUV—Henry had headed off in Gerard's SUV to Dunedin airport—and walked the four car lengths to Storm in a Teacup. It was a pretty building, surrounded by flowers. Several customers sat drinking coffee on the front verandah while inside, he could see a line waiting for service.

The doorbell tinkled as he entered, and myriad scents wrapped around his senses. He joined the end of the line for service. Coffee. Baking scents—something with golden syrup, if he wasn't mistaken. The pungent scent of green herbs. A rose scent from the lady in front of him in the line. Orange blossom...

Everything in him froze and time seemed to still as he scanned the seats inside the café.

Megan Saxon was sitting in the corner at a table by herself. While he gaped at her, his wolf telling him to stake a claim, she glanced up and spotted him. She recognized him straightaway, tension sliding through her shoulders to match his own. He watched her throat work in a swallow and cursed his timing. He should've waited until later when the café wouldn't be so busy. The truth—he liked London and wanted to have the welcome-home treat on hand as Henry had suggested, especially since he'd share their home for the foreseeable future.

Bad call.

She wanted Henry, and Jacey didn't need another rejection. His ego had already suffered enough. He jerked his attention away and focused on the line of customers in front of him, willing them to stop procrastinating over their orders.

The scent of orange blossom became stronger, the tints of cinnamon and wolf sharper. Jacey had to wrestle with his wolf, fight for control. A tremor racked his muscles.

"Excuse me," a hesitant voice said.

A hand tapped his forearm, the slight contact like an electrical current passing through his body. It rocked him and blew away his resolution to avoid the woman.

Slowly, slowly he turned to face Megan Saxon.

She swallowed again, her cheeks pale as she faced him. "I-I thought I recognized you. I-I want..." She cleared her throat. "Can I buy you a coffee to apologize for my behavior last night? I-I..." Her shoulders slumped, and she glanced at her boots. Then she squared her shoulders and forced herself to meet his gaze. "I have no excuse for my bad behavior, but obviously, I shouldn't drink red wine on an empty stomach. What do you say? Can I buy you a coffee and a muffin?"

Jacey nodded, even though he thought this was a bad idea.

"Um, I don't even know your name." She thrust out her hand. "My name is Megan Saxon."

"Jacey Anderson." His hand grasped hers but he let go as soon as possible.

"Sit at my table. It's the one in the corner over there. Would you like a muffin to go with your coffee? The blueberry ones are delicious."

"A chocolate brownie, please," Jacey said. He could do this. Drink a cup of coffee with the woman, accept her apology and move on with his life.

She slipped into his place in the line and waved him away. "I won't be long."

Bemused, Jacey maneuvered his way through the busy café, past tables of families, two gossiping grannies, rounded two strollers and a discarded doll. He pulled out the spare chair at the table and wondered how long he should stay to be polite. Anything longer than that would be self-torture.

Megan glanced over her shoulder at the man. In broad daylight, she could see how attractive he was with his silver hair, his fit body and those piercing blue eyes that seemed to see right through her to her acute embarrassment. Age—she'd guess five, maybe ten years older than her, yet he hadn't let himself go. Those faded jeans of his showcased muscular thighs and a tight butt. A real silver fox. Her girlfriends—the few she kept in touch with, but didn't get to see as much as she liked because they lived in different parts of the world—would go gaga over him.

On reaching the counter, she placed her order and realized she hadn't asked what sort of coffee he wanted. Most men preferred something plain.

"Jacey drinks black coffee," Emily said. "I didn't realize you knew anyone here in Middlemarch."

"Ah, I met him last night and owed him a drink. I like to pay my debts."

Emily nodded. "I'll be another ten minutes. Do you want to reschedule for this afternoon?"

"No, it's fine." She handed over money to pay for the order.

When she walked over to her table, she noticed Jacey playing with a toddler at the next table. He differed from the men in her workplace, most of whom would brush off a kid in a café. They only deigned to deal with the youngsters who had something to do with their latest assignment.

She pulled out her chair and slipped onto the seat, unaccountably nervous. "Emily told me you drink black coffee. Sorry. I focused on apologizing and didn't ask for your preference. I owe an apology to the other man with you last night, an even bigger one."

"My son, Henry."

Oh, god. Her stomach seemed to swoop to her boots. She hadn't remembered that bit. "I'm so sorry. What must you think of me?" She bit her lip. "I suppose I behaved badly with a married man?" Another question popped up. "Did I hear you say you were staying at the cottage?"

"Our company provides security for Gilcrest. We were there to check the lighting." He stared at her, his gaze piercing, dissecting. "Henry is single."

And you? She wanted to ask but bit down on her bottom lip to halt the question. After making a fool of herself already, it was best she censor her curiosity.

"His girlfriend died, murdered by her ex-husband. Although you're embarrassed, the kiss jerked Henry from his misery, even if it was for a short time. I worry about my son."

"Oh. I'm sorry. That must be difficult. At least he has you and his mother to support him."

"My wife died when Henry was twelve."

Megan stared at Jacey, her stomach churning and a prickle of heat rushed across her face, down her neck and back. Could she do anything right with this man? "I'm so sorry," she blurted, unable to meet his gaze. "I seem to keep putting my foot in my mouth with you. Oh, here's the coffee and the brownie. Thank goodness. It will save me from another faux pas."

"Emily made a fresh cup for you too," the waitress said. "She said to tell you she won't be much longer."

"Could you get Emily to put away a dozen chocolate brownies? Gerard and London are coming home today."

"Great! We miss London around here."

"I'll pay for the brownies on my way out."

"Okay." The waitress cleared the table of empty cups and plates and disappeared behind the counter.

Megan sighed, waiting for Jacey's reaction to her blurting. Really, her friends and colleagues would wet themselves laughing if they were witness to this awkward encounter.

When he didn't reply, that told her everything. She still couldn't look at the man. There was something about him that tugged at her senses, made her want to get him to like her, but she didn't trust her instincts at present.

Smiling at the waitress, she sucked in a deep breath and stilled. His scent. It was the same one from last night. A mixture of ginger and...and mulled wine, yet the fragrance reminded her of the outdoors too. Someone should bottle the decadent aroma and sell it. They'd make a fortune. A pang of reluctance filled her at the idea. Good grief. What was wrong with her? A three-day weekend tournament, remember? After last night's mess, she'd refine Plan B to keep herself out of trouble.

No men.

Much safer.

"You can look at me. I won't bite."

Maybe she wanted him to take a nip or two. She shook her head and raised her gaze so it struck the top of the table and her fresh cup of coffee.

"You haven't upset me. Moira...well, it was a long time ago."

"It must've been difficult for you to raise a son on your own."

"We muddled along," Jacey said, and he placed his hand on top of hers.

Megan jumped at the physical contact, memories of Charlie flooding her mind. She still remembered the breathless anticipation she'd felt when he'd curled his fingers around hers. Jacey's innocent touch sent an equal burst of energy sizzling across her skin. Her gaze shot to his, and she encountered good humor and understanding.

He smiled, and her breath caught, that annoying prickling firing to life again. She tried. She attempted to hold his gaze. The seconds lengthened, and when she managed to gasp a breath, that ginger and mulled wine, along with the green and wildness of the outdoors flooded her with dizziness. She gasped at the physical awareness that sprang to life in her body—her breasts and her rapid heartbeat—and wrested her gaze free.

With a trembling hand, she reached for her latte. The milky coffee sloshed over the rim of her cup and, mortified, she set her drink down with a clink and seized a napkin.

"Do I make you nervous?"

The wretched man sounded pleased.

"No," she snapped and blotted the splashes on her notebook. The table shook with the force of her dabs.

"You make *me* nervous."

The confession drew her, and she risked a glance. His broad grin drew a frown. "You're laughing at me."

"No. Taste the brownie and tell me what you think. They're London's favorite."

"Is London your girlfriend?"

"No," he said. "Henry's best friend, Gerard, is married to London. They're arriving home today from their honeymoon."

"Oh."

"Gerard is like a second son. He and Henry have been friends since their school days. Gerard and London married in Fiji. Henry and I were there for their wedding but came back early to give the newlyweds privacy. Go on. Try the brownie."

"But it's yours."

Jacey picked up his coffee spoon and used it to separate the brownie into two even pieces. "There you go. Now it's ours."

Megan accepted the brownie and took a bite. Chocolate and sweetness danced across her taste buds. She swallowed. Delicious. "I can see why London would love these."

"You have chocolate..." His blue eyes gleamed.

Self-consciously, she wiped at her mouth.

"No, let me," he said, his voice husky and compelling.

He picked up a napkin and wiped her bottom lip.

"There you go," he said.

"Am I interrupting?" An amused Emily Mitchell stood beside their table. Curiosity blazed in her expression before it blanked. Or had that been smugness?

Megan shook herself and when she looked again, all she saw was a friendly smile.

"Not at all." Jacey rose. "I need to get going. I promised Henry I'd do errands for him. Thanks for your company, Ms. Saxon."

"Rachel should have your brownies ready for you at the counter," Emily said.

"Thanks." Jacey strode toward the counter, and Megan's gaze followed along like a pet lamb. The man looked perfect from all angles.

"Nice butt."

"Yes," Megan agreed absently before she registered what

she'd said. "Oh. I didn't say that."

Emily laughed, patted her hand and claimed the seat Jacey had vacated. "He's single if you're interested. I don't know him well since he's new to Middlemarch but his son, Henry, is lovely."

"Are you kidding? My schedule is so full I barely have time to think, let alone attempt any relationship."

Emily cocked her head like an inquisitive bird. "That must be lonely."

A hit. Megan refused to let her emotions free and forced herself to sit straight, to choke back the heavy sigh struggling for release. This was the path she'd chosen to survive losing Charlie, and she had to own it.

"Could you give me a little background about the two teams who are playing the opening match for the Sevens tournament tonight?" Megan glanced through the details her boss had forwarded to her. "I've got the list of players, and I see you've given me a brief bio. That's good. I can have fun with these details. My boss has also asked me to do a special-interest piece on Middlemarch. It will go in our subscriber magazine plus my report about the tournament. I believe it's the first one you've held. Why did you decide to hold a Sevens tournament?"

"We want to entice our young people to stay in the region or come back on a regular basis to take part in local functions. A few years ago, the town of Middlemarch was dying. They had a shortage of young women and lots of single men who stayed here to farm the land. We wanted a better balance and to make Middlemarch a fun place to live. We've organized dances, have a regular weekend market, hold self-defense courses for all age groups, and have a boot camp. Two months ago, we had a zombie run, which was so popular, we intend to hold another one next year."

Emily Mitchell's enthusiasm for her hometown shone through her words.

"I'll interview some of the players and supporters tonight and during the rest of the tournament," Megan said as she jotted notes in her own particular shorthand.

"That sounds good," Emily said. "I have to thank you again for agreeing to come to our event. I feel guilty when you've said how busy you are."

"Don't. I didn't mean to sound as if I didn't want to be here." She didn't, but it was no excuse for rudeness.

"I heard rumors you will be one of the hosts for the new show they're advertising."

"No," Megan said and pushed away the stab of disappointment. "Just rumors. Was there anything else you needed me to take care of? Any particular people I should mention."

"One of our locals died recently, and we've named the winners' cup in his honor. Would you be able to present the cup to the winning team and read a short speech about Kenneth Nesbitt? I'd ask a local to do it but anyone I ask would have been close to Kenneth and they might break down speaking in public. We want this to be a celebration of his life and a way to remember him."

"Not a problem. I'd be honored," Megan said.

"There is one more thing," Emily said. "We're always fundraising. This time it is for new sports equipment for the local school. The organizing committee wondered if you would donate some of your time, so we could auction off a date with you."

Megan opened her mouth to refuse and Emily Mitchell spoke faster, not giving her a chance to object.

"The winner would take you on a date for dinner here at the café. We thought an early dinner in case the winner is a youngster. We have both girls and boys who play Sevens rugby at school, and I know they're all keen to say hello to you and quiz you about your job. Will you do it?"

As if she had any choice. Megan forced a smile. "I'd be happy to." A couple of hours. It wouldn't be too bad, and it wasn't as if she hadn't donated her time in a similar fashion before.

LATER THAT NIGHT, JACEY trailed Henry as they walked into the Middlemarch school hall for the opening ceremony.

Henry scanned the rows of seats, all occupied. "Looks like standing room only."

"Hey, mister. Want to buy a raffle ticket?" a perky teenage girl asked. Her friend, a giggly blonde with pigtails, shook a container of money in front of Jacey's face.

"How much?" Jacey asked.

"Ten dollars a ticket or three for twenty dollars."

"I've got it," Henry said, pulling a twenty out of his wallet.

"You need to write your name on the tickets, mister," the

girl said to Henry.

Henry took care of the ticket formalities for both of them and shoved the tickets in his pocket.

"Thanks," the two teenagers chorused, and they moved on to their next victims.

"Leo and Isabella are waving at us," Jacey said.

"Good, they've saved us seats." Henry wove through the knots of locals, exchanging a word here and there and ignoring the whispers from the anti-wolf felines who were brave enough to voice their opposition.

Jacey ignored them too, his belly swirling in anticipation. Tonight they'd see Megan Saxon again. He wasn't sure what to do about Megan. This morning, his presence had unsettled her and he'd witnessed the dawning awareness in her blue eyes. The attraction wasn't just on his side, but he wasn't sure...

No, not true. He and his wolf were in total agreement. They should grab her, take her to a private place and get horizontal, although vertical against a door or a wall would work equally well. As long as he got his hands on her, he wasn't fussy.

Saber Mitchell appeared on the stage at the front of the hall and raised his right hand for silence.

"Are Gerard and London coming?" Isabella asked.

"They'll be along later, in time for the opening match," Henry said. "London wanted to unpack first."

Up on the stage, Saber tapped on the mic and started speaking. "I'd like to welcome everyone to the inaugural Kenneth Nesbitt Sevens tournament. Most of you have seen or heard of our guest commentator since she has graced our screens and introduced us to different sports for the last ten years. I'd like you all to put your hands together to welcome, Megan Saxon."

A thunderous applause filled the hall as Megan strode onto the stage. Jacey clapped with the rest of the audience. He leaned back in his hard chair and watched her with a great deal of pleasure. She wore a charcoal-gray pantsuit with a red scarf around her neck. Her high heels clicked on the wood stage with each confident step. Once she reached Saber Mitchell, she shook his hand and turned to beam at the audience.

"Welcome to the inaugural Kenneth Nesbitt Sevens tournament. I'm thrilled to be here in the capacity of commentator, and I look forward to seeing what you can all do on the rugby field. But first, I'd like to pay homage to one of your homegrown heroes, Kenneth Nesbitt."

The crowd listened as Megan told them of the big man with the big heart who loved learning new things, including using his smartphone. She mentioned how he'd turned up in Middlemarch as a five-year-old and stood up to the three bullies trying to shove Benjamin Urquart and Sid Blackburn into a thorny hedge. That was the beginning of a lifelong friendship.

By the time Megan finished there wasn't a dry eye in the hall. Jacey hadn't met the man, but pride filled him at the way Megan had portrayed him.

"So I want you to play hard and play fair in the spirit of Kenneth Nesbitt. May the best team win!" Megan beamed at the applause, waited until the din died. "I now declare the Kenneth Nesbitt Sevens tournament open. Let's play rugby!"

"She's good," Henry murmured.

"Yes."

"One last thing before we start the opening match," Saber said. "Megan graciously allowed us to raffle off a date with her, with the proceeds going toward new sports equipment for the school. The lucky winner will have the honor of dining with Megan at Storm in a Teacup tomorrow night." He flashed a broad grin. "I know the owner and the food is exceptional."

Everyone laughed.

"Right. Emily, I'll get you to draw the winner," Saber said.

Emily thrust her hand into a bag and pulled out one yellow raffle ticket. She handed it to Saber.

"And the winner of a dinner date at Storm in a Teacup with Megan Saxon is Jacey Anderson. Jacey, come and see Emily later this evening, and she'll let you know more about your date."

Jacey stared at Emily and Saber, feeling a frown dig into his cheeks. Henry clapped him on the back. Leo and Isabella both stood ready to leave the hall.

"Congratulations, Jacey," Isabella said. "You'll be the envy of a lot of Middlemarch men. Megan Saxon might be in her forties but she's one sexy lady."

Jacey nodded and turned his focus on Henry and Leo. "Did you do this?"

"I bought tickets and wrote your name on them," Henry said. "That's all."

When Henry had been a child, Jacey had known

whenever he was lying or had taken part in a mischievous act. At some stage, Henry had acquired an impassive face, and annoyingly, he couldn't tell if his son was telling him what he wanted to hear or the truth. Jacey turned his gaze to Leo. Leo wore the same enigmatic expression, which raised Jacey's bull-crap register.

"Maybe I could donate the prize back and they could raffle it off again."

"No," Henry snapped. "You won fair and square. The method we discussed yesterday—it didn't go down that way."

"Nope," Leo added. "This was plain, dumb luck."

Henry glared at him. "A sign that this is worth exploring."

Jacey snorted. "The lady kissed you, not me."

"I didn't encourage her."

"Did we miss something?" Isabella asked.

"No," Jacey said, fervently wishing he hadn't raised the subject.

"Yes." Leo peered at them both. "I wasn't present during any kissing."

Most of the crowd had dispersed, going outside to stake out their places on the sideline.

"Just as well," Isabella said in a tart voice. "A mate doesn't like to hear this sort of thing."

"Jacey, you like her." Henry's gaze drilled into him. "Stop putting up roadblocks. It's just dinner."

Wrong. It was more because during their cup of coffee this morning things had clicked between them. Unfortunately, once he'd left, he'd realized his wolf

75

couldn't keep her—not when she was a public figure.

"You're right," he said. "It's just dinner. I can deal with one dinner." But the truth. He wasn't sure he could keep his hands off her.

THE NEXT NIGHT, Storm in a Teacup

The first day of the Sevens tournament had passed so quickly. She'd laughed, joked, and had fun commentating the games that took place on the main field. The local team was doing well, and she hoped she kept her favoritism hidden.

"Megan," Emily said. "You're early. Your table is over here." She gestured to a private corner, partially screened with plants so the table wasn't visible to the entire café. "Would you like a glass of wine while you wait?"

Megan considered her answer. It would help with her nerves because she was apprehensive about seeing Jacey again. On the other hand, too much wine wasn't good.

"Hard question?" Emily teased.

"I'd love a glass of wine," Megan said with dignity as she took a seat at the table. "White please." The red wine had got her into trouble.

"One glass of wine coming up," Emily said. "Are you tired? You've been working nonstop all day."

"I'm used to it. With my job, it's all fast-paced. I don't know any other way."

"What about your down time? And all the travel you do? That must be tedious at times."

"I catch up on sleep, watch movies. Read books." And wrote paranormal romances to fill the lonely hours after she'd discovered that some men dated her so they could say they'd slept with a celebrity. Sometimes, those wolves were difficult to spot, and she'd discovered that to her cost.

"Ah, Jacey, you're here," Emily said. "Would you like a glass of wine or a beer?"

"A beer please." Jacey waited until Emily disappeared before turning to her. His gaze swept her, and her skin tingled as if he'd run his fingers down her spine. "I'd decided I wouldn't see you again."

An arrow of hurt struck near her heart, and she stared at him, floundering for a reply.

The silence lengthened until it made her want to fidget. Her, who'd had all the fidget knocked out of her by bossy TV producers.

"Why?" Not what she'd intended to say, but she craved an answer. Why didn't he want to see her again? Was it the wine episode? Or the fact she'd foisted herself on his son?

Jacey pulled out the seat opposite her and sat. "Because I wanted to take you home with me, and I don't think that's a good idea. You're a public figure. I like my privacy. The last thing I want is to find myself in a ladies' magazine or the newspaper."

"Like my previous boyfriends?"

"I looked you up on the internet."

"You can't believe everything you read on the web."

"I know that." His gaze was steady.

"We could make a pact to have two nights together. Two private nights where no one except us would even know

77

we were together."

Jacey sucked in a sharp breath, his only reaction to her proposition. Goodness, had she blundered yet again?

"Jacey?"

A slow grin curled across his sensual lips, and those blue eyes of his glowed in a freaky manner. "Do you go around propositioning men, Ms. Saxon?"

"No!" She covered her face with her hands, silently regretting kissing Jacey's son yet again. A moment of sheer madness. She blamed Janet for planting the younger man idea into her head.

She uncovered her face, placing one clenched hand in her lap and the other palm flat on the tabletop. "I said I don't go around kissing strange men. It was a mistake and one I bitterly regret. I'd take it back if I could."

He reached across the table and placed his hand on top of hers. "I believe you."

"You do?"

"Yes. What do you say about a picnic instead of having dinner here with the nosy locals?"

Megan had already noticed the interest they were attracting with their conversation from those diners who could see them despite the plants. "Won't that cause more gossip? And won't the locals talk to anyone who asks?"

"You're right. So we sit here and eat our meals, then we go our separate ways."

"And meet at my cottage?" she asked.

"We could do that if you're sure."

She started to speak, but he squeezed her hand. "Here comes Emily with our drinks. How did you get into your job?"

She blinked at him and mourned the loss of contact when he removed his hand. She hadn't even heard Emily's arrival, which told her he'd seduced her with his baby blues, his crooked grin and his stunning silver hair. Then, there was his easygoing nature and his obvious love for his son. Emily handed her a glass of white wine and Jacey his beer before offering them a menu bearing the evening dishes.

"I'll be back in a few minutes," Emily said and bustled away.

"If you looked me up on the internet, then you know all that. Tell me about you. I got the impression you haven't been in Middlemarch for long. Why did you move?"

"Henry needed me," Jacey said.

Surprise heralded his reply and her curiosity grew. "He's an adult." Few men would change their lives and move because their child—an adult child—needed them.

"He's still my son and when his m-girlfriend died the local cops blamed him. He didn't do it, but they refused to listen. Besides, the business in Perth wasn't a challenge any longer. Henry and Gerard have been asking me to come and help them with their new security firm. They seem to have plenty of work coming in, so I said I'd come back to New Zealand and Middlemarch for a trial period."

Her reporter instincts flared to life. Maybe she, too, should hit the internet in pursuit of knowledge. Wrongful imprisonment and murder bore the hallmarks of an interesting story.

"Have you ever been married? Had a serious

relationship?"

Her eyes widened at the abrupt change of topic. "Whoa, you don't ease into these things, do you?"

"I want to know the answer if we're going to spend time together."

"Relationships are difficult with my job. During the rugby season, I travel a lot. In the off-season, I travel just as often to film segments for different shows." At least she used to be away from home on a regular basis. Who knew what would happen once she reported in with her boss again. "Most men prefer their women in the same place as them. It makes dating easier. Sex too."

His gaze narrowed. "You enjoy sex?"

"Yes." She refused to let him rattle her, yet his bluntness was kind of inspiring. Endearing even, as if he didn't go for pretense and games.

"So do I," he murmured. "Do you just do television work?"

Another change of subject. She groped to keep up because her mind had become stuck on sex. Naked bodies writhing together, urgency humming between them. The cool night air. The beautiful pearly shine of the moon. The mournful howl... She blinked. Once. Twice.

"Megan?" His soft voice pulled her back. "Woolgathering? That's not very flattering."

"I..." She shook her head to clear her sluggish thoughts. That was the first time she'd drifted into her fictional world while in the presence of a sexy man. Heck, in the presence of any man. "Sorry, the sex discussion threw me. I'm not used to forthright speaking. The last man I dated—he was very economical with the truth. He forgot to tell me about the other two women he was dating at the same time as me. He didn't tell the other two women either, so it was a rude shock when we all turned up on the same night."

Jacey barked out a laugh. "Sorry. I know it's not funny, but the picture in my mind had all the hallmarks of a comedy."

Megan gave a rueful smile. "It's funny now. It wasn't at the time. One woman had a short fuse and picked up someone's pasta dinner. She fired it at the man's head, missed and splattered spaghetti all over the second woman. It turned out she had a temper too. In seconds it was all on. A food fight that made headlines. My workmates still crack jokes at my expense, and that was over two years ago."

His lips twitched. "Did you join in?"

"No, I had a little self-preservation. I attempted to make a discreet exit, but these days everyone has a cell phone. Most of the videos went viral. Lucky, there were a few other celebrities present, some of whom threw their food."

"I might have come across the video during my internet search. You behaved with dignity, and public opinion was behind you."

"Try telling my conservative bosses. Although ratings rose after the incident." She lifted her hands to emphasize the word incident with air-speech marks.

Jacey chuckled. "Emily is on her way. Have you decided what you'd like to eat for dinner?"

Megan picked up her menu, gave it a quick scan since now that Jacey mentioned it, she could pick out Emily's approach.

"Have you decided?" Emily asked as she popped around the temporary screen comprising flowering plants on a decorative bookshelf.

"That's easy," Megan said. "Roast beef."

"I cook it on the rare side, although I could manage medium rare for you."

"No, rare is how I like my meat." And everyone looked at her strangely whenever she ordered a rare steak instead of a healthy salad or the latest trendy food item.

"I'll take the same, thanks, Emily," Jacey said.

Emily turned to leave, then stopped, her brow furrowed. "I should tell you that several reporters have turned up, searching for you, Megan. They said it's about a new sports show and you missing out on a job." She pulled a face. "Sorry for my bluntness, but I thought you'd prefer to have the facts."

Megan sighed, a part of her knowing that this would happen when management made their announcement about the front people for their new show. Although, she didn't know how the reporters had discovered her presence in Middlemarch. Someone at the main network office must've blabbed, which meant her relaxing weekend would be no longer. She sighed again and forced a smile. "It's all right. Occupational hazard." She didn't intend to explain her disappointment or anger at the way the network bosses were pushing her aside because of her age.

"Don't worry. We'll sneak you out the back when you're ready to leave," Emily said.

Megan nodded, searing anger filling her, aimed at Jeremy and the network bosses. If she kicked up a stink and let her disappointment show to reporters and the public, it would only up interest in the new show. The reporters would speak of a war between her and the girl who'd snatched her job. Been there, and she didn't care to repeat the experience. No matter what she said, she'd appear bitter. Best to keep to the old favorite, *no comment.*

The roast beef, when it arrived, melted in her mouth. Accompanied by crisp roast potatoes, pumpkin and kumara, her favorite sweet potato, green beans and gravy, the meal reminded her of dinners at her grandparents' farm north of Auckland during her childhood.

"Do the reporters create a nuisance for you?"

"Sometimes," Megan said. "It's part of the job. I like meeting fellow sports enthusiasts, but dealing with the press is always a balancing act. It's hard because I'm also a reporter working on stories, except my stories aren't print. Anyone who works in the public arena is open season."

A shudder tore through her at the thought. Thank goodness she'd kept her penname of Carrie English secret. Now that would be a disaster. She could imagine the controversy if that little secret got out. The love scenes read aloud out of context, the pointed stares and sniggers from her workmates. Even her younger sister would look askance. Megan knew this, had experienced this prejudice against romance from her own sister because Tessa had picked up one of her Carrie English paranormal romances and mocked the cover. Mocked it! She'd flicked through the pages and read out a love scene, one Megan had been proud of and finished by demanding why Megan read such rubbish.

The memory still burned. Her sister's loss. That cover…if she ever came across a man with abs like that she'd lick them, not mock them. And if she ever found a lover who took such care to arouse her, she'd grab him with both hands and never let him go. The men she met had faulty parts. Oh, their favorite, requisite male parts worked fine. It was the parts that came under *other* that failed to fire Megan's imagination.

"Hey!"

Megan jumped as a hand touched hers. She glanced up, her gaze connecting with concerned blue eyes.

"It will be fine. I'm experienced in security work, as are Henry and Gerard. Any or all of us will make sure you're not bothered for the rest of the weekend."

Megan laughed, at herself more than at his words. "This is a big juicy story, Jacey. It will be better if I speak with them and hopefully, they'll go away."

"Whatever you decide is best. What I'm saying is we'll help you control the situation."

He meant it. This man who hardly knew her. Something inside her cracked a little, releasing some of her frustration and anger. She blew out a breath and pushed away her empty plate.

"A few days ago, my boss called me into his office to tell me that the job they'd promised me has been given to another woman."

Jacey's brow furrowed. "Why?"

"My age. They decided I was too old for the job, that my competence and experience and good work record to date didn't matter a scrap."

Jacey stared, the furrow deepening on his forehead. "They have rocks for brains." A low growl accompanied the words. "Anyone seeing you in action this weekend would say the same."

A surge of warmth dampened her frustration. "Thanks."

"What are you going to do?"

A harsh sigh gusted from her—definitely vexation in that one. "I don't know. I've taken a week of leave and hope to have a brainwave as to what I should do next. I have a couple of options and still have my job at the moment. They're shunting me sideways, so I'm not sure what my job will entail going forward. I've started a list of pros and cons to work out what I want, but it's scary trying to imagine a future without sport. Sport has been such a big part of my life—ever since I played rugby for the New Zealand Women's Sevens team. Actually before that, since I was a kid."

"Your passion for the game shows," Jacey said. "I enjoyed watching you in action today. Thanks to you, the tournament is very successful."

"Your local team is good. I'm picking them to win the Kenneth Nesbitt cup," she said, glowing inside with his compliments. "I'll admit I was miffed to be given this assignment because I'd never heard of Middlemarch, but everyone has made me welcome, and I've enjoyed the local revelry. There is a real spirit of friendship and community in this town."

"It's part of the reason I decided to stay," Jacey said. "I've only lived here for a short time, but the residents look out for each other. I think I would have stayed because of Henry and his friend, Gerard, anyway, but the community spirit is a plus."

Emily appeared around the corner of the screen. "Ah good. I can see the roast beef went down well."

"Are the reporters still there?" Megan asked.

Emily scowled. "I had to get Saber to man the door, so only customers can get inside. They have the manners of a three-year-old. No, scratch that. Most three-year-olds of my acquaintance have better manners."

A grin surfaced in Megan, surprising her by its appearance. She'd liked Emily Mitchell from their first meeting. The men and women on the organizing committee had made her welcome too, although the two elderly women on the committee were scary. She kept that opinion to herself. "They're a tenacious lot. They'll stay until I leave."

"We'll hustle you out the back."

Megan straightened in her chair. "No, I'll go out the front and give a short statement. If I don't, they'll haunt me tomorrow and perhaps spoil things for the final day of the tournament."

Emily shot her a considering glance then gave a brisk nod. "If that's what you want to do. Jacey and Saber will act as your security and keep things orderly. She grinned. "I don't think we've ever had a press conference in Middlemarch." She picked up the plates. "I'll give you a break before dessert, but we have a lemon tart or a molten chocolate cake."

"Yum," Megan said. "My favorites. You expect me to

choose?"

Jacey gave a husky laugh. "We'll have one of each, Emily, so we can share."

"Done deal," Emily said and departed with the empty plates.

Megan focused on Jacey, her heart beating faster than normal. There was so much to like about this man. One, he was attractive. Two, he had manners and didn't monopolize the conversation. Three, he was protective without being creepy. Four, he didn't comment about her love of food and in particular, bloody meat. Five, his grin was a panty-wetting one.

Words bubbled from her and she blurted, "I should've kissed you instead of your son."

CHAPTER SIX

"READY?" JACEY ASKED. *I should have kissed you instead of your son*. The words played on a loop like a favorite song, and his wolf wanted to sing in concert.

Megan nodded, and Saber opened the front door of Storm in a Teacup.

The reporters talked at once, firing questions at Megan as she followed Saber from the café. The clamor rose above the tinkle of the doorbell, swelling yet again as Jacey placed himself on one side of her and Saber on the other.

A growl rumbled from him as he felt Megan tremble. Saber didn't have to shoot him the *look* for him to clamp down on his wolf. More than ever, he felt he and Megan had a future together. He didn't want to utter the M word since Megan didn't sense the ties between them, but his wolf was acting mighty possessive.

"Megan! Megan!" A skinny man with a ponytail and wearing a bright orange T-shirt and black jeans thrust a fluffy microphone in her face.

Megan ignored the shouts for her attention, lifted her right hand for silence and waited, fully composed.

Pride surged in Jacey. After the tremors when they exited the café, she'd reached a place of calm and displayed no nerves or outward signs of distaste for this debacle. He wasn't sure he would manage the same composure because his wolf kept bleeding out with inward growls that were increasingly distracting.

When the din continued, Jacey stepped forward and spoke in a carrying voice. "Ms. Saxon will have no comment until you cease your rude chatter."

Silence fell, and in a comical pause, everyone eyed him with curiosity and calculation. *Who are you?* Jacey could hear them thinking the question.

"Thank you," Megan said. "I presume you are here to cover the Inaugural Kenneth Nesbitt Sevens tournament. I am honored to commentate the games. The rugby has been entertaining, the competing teams playing hard. I think the crowd has enjoyed the spectacle. I know I have."

Jacey heard Saber's chuckle, quickly silenced. Megan knew the reporters were here for her, but she'd used the opportunity to give the Sevens tournament a plug. He hoped that this made the papers because although visitors meant possible exposure, the tourist dollars meant the town flourished.

"Is it true that Rowena Tichmarsh has stolen your job on the new sports show with Dallas Jones?" someone shouted from the rear of the crowd.

Megan smiled, although Jacey felt her inner tension.

89

"My name was one of several in the running for the job. The network chose Rowena as the best candidate for the position, and I know she'll do an excellent job. As you all know, I love sports. All sports, so I'm looking forward to seeing the show on our screens."

"How do you feel about the network choosing someone younger for the job?"

Megan smiled again. "I don't believe age came into the equation. The network chose the candidate they felt fit with their vision for the show. That is all."

"Who is the man you had dinner with? Is he your new boyfriend? Will there be any food fights?" a woman shouted above the other reporters.

"I believe I can answer that," Saber said. "Mr. Anderson won a raffle for dinner with Ms. Saxon. The raffle funds are going toward new sports equipment for Middlemarch School. We're still accepting donations if any of you are interested in contributing to this worthwhile cause."

"What did you talk about?" a woman asked Jacey.

"We discussed sports and rugby, skiing in Queenstown and the Middlemarch Rail trail. Oh, and we talked about roast beef because Storm in the Teacup does an excellent roast dinner. I recommend it," Jacey said. "Also we argued about whether chocolate cake or lemon tart should come first on the top five dessert choices."

"Megan, what did you vote for?" the woman asked. "Chocolate or lemon?"

"I'm afraid our argument remained unsettled since I couldn't decide," Megan said with a laugh.

"Megan, do you feel any anger toward Rowena for

stealing your job?"

"No, not at all. Rowena will make an excellent host for the show," Megan said.

"What are you going to do now?" a man shouted. "They've replaced you on the commentating team."

"I have several options, which I will consider. Thank you, ladies and gentlemen. That is all."

Saber stepped in front of Megan and pushed his way through the jostling reporters and cameramen. Jacey followed Megan, making sure that no one grabbed her or attempted to interfere in her departure.

They escorted Megan to her rental car and held the crowd back as she drove away. She'd be safe from reporters once she entered Gilcrest Station.

"How come you and Henry were there last night if security is so good?" she'd demanded when he and Saber had discussed their plans to handle the reporters and her departure from the café.

"One of the security lights was playing up, and we wanted to see it at night. The owner told us it wasn't coming on as it should, but we couldn't find anything wrong when we tested it during the day," Jacey had said.

Megan had seemed satisfied with the explanation.

Jacey watched Megan drive away and itched to follow. They'd both agreed that he should leave it an hour before he visited her to give the reporters time to settle and hopefully leave. As Emily had pointed out to him, the reporters wouldn't find anywhere to stay and would have to drive to one of the surrounding towns or back to Dunedin for accommodation.

"Come back to the café for a drink," Saber offered. "It will make the waiting easier."

"Emily spread the gossip already?"

"What gossip?" Saber asked in a mild voice. "It was clear to me there is something between the two of you. She's cool and professional. I doubt any of the reporters picked up on your mutual attraction."

Jacey wanted to ask questions but shrugged instead. His business. Megan's business. No one else needed to know a thing. "A drink sounds good."

Inside the café, Emily directed him and Saber to the same table where he and Megan had sat. The screen had gone, leaving the table visible to everyone who entered. The café was just as busy and now that tables were freeing up, Emily let in the reporters who wanted to buy coffee or dinner. Jacey noted that she directed them to tables away from him and Saber.

"A beer?" Saber asked.

"I could do with another coffee."

"Coming right up," Emily said. "I'd join you but business is brisker than I thought it would be." The doorbell tinkled, and Emily beamed. "Ching-ching. I love the sound of money."

Saber grinned after his mate before turning back to Jacey. "Did you get that matter sorted? I presumed you did since I heard nothing else."

"Two incriminating photos deleted," Jacey said. "I don't think she even looked at them. It was just bad luck on our part to be in the wrong place at the wrong time."

"Thank you for taking care of it," Saber said. "It

would've been difficult to explain to a council meeting why my brother and a new member of the community had outed us to the world at large."

"Do you think there will ever come a time when we come out to the public?" Jacey asked.

Saber appeared troubled at the question. "Logic dictates we must, and I've heard whispers the other paranormal races feel the same way. The human race though, they're not ready for the knowledge. I watch the news, see the way they shoot and kill each other..." He shook his head. "All we can do is make strong ties with our community and prepare for the day when exposure becomes inevitable."

Jacey's respect and liking for the younger man increased on hearing those words, and it underlined his decision to move to Middlemarch as a good one. He, too, believed the time would come when they'd walk openly amongst the human race. The werewolf community in Perth didn't embrace the future, being old-fashioned and unprepared. Nothing would be easy about the announcement, and it would need to be managed to prevent panic amongst the humans. Strong men like Saber Mitchell would help make the transition easier.

"Do you have a contingency plan?"

"Not yet, but I've been thinking we should develop one," Saber said. "Concealment is more difficult with a denser population. It's not like the days of the past when communication took days. These days it is instant, and that can work against us. A plan is a good idea."

"If there is any way I can help, please let me know. Henry and I are both moon called. We have to shift on a regular basis to control our wolf. It's inevitable that someone will spy on us or see us, given the encroachment of towns and cities on the wilderness spaces."

"Exactly. I need to convince everyone on the council of this and get them to agree to a worst-case scenario plan. How are you going to get to Ms. Saxon's place without the press noticing?"

Jacey stared at Saber. "Not sure of the logistics yet. It depends on the reporters. I saw none of them following her, but if they have, they won't get past the gates. I can shift to wolf and sneak in, but then Megan will ask questions about how I got there without a vehicle."

Ten minutes later, with unexpected nerves doing a jig in the pit of his stomach, Jacey drove toward Gilcrest Station. The country roads lay in darkness, lit only by a lackluster moon and his headlights, and he didn't pass a single vehicle. He slowed for the entranceway, pleased to see not one thing out of place. Not a car. Not a reporter.

It was easy to open the gate using the passkey George Gilcrest had given Henry. Henry had asked him to deliver it back to the owner, and he'd do that tomorrow morning. He drove through the landscaped gardens, illuminated by the security lights, and headed for Megan's cottage. He parked beside her zippy red rental, a sense of exhilaration pushing his mouth into a smile.

The instant he tapped on the door, it flew open. Megan grabbed his hand and dragged him inside. Her gaze darted left and darted right before she slammed the door behind him. "Did anyone see you?"

"No, the reporters stayed in town."

"Did they take your photo?"

"No, why would they?"

Megan scowled. "To put with the story about me and Rowena. Something about a romance always ups ratings."

"Are you ashamed of being with me?" Even Jacey heard the testy note in his tone. "We have done nothing yet, so I can always leave and go home. While I don't mind keeping to the background, I will not hide either."

Crap. She'd upset him, and that wasn't what she meant to do at all. Those reporters and their stupid questions had rattled her when she should be used to their methods by this stage in her career.

"Megan, do you want me to leave?"

She blinked, dragged back to the present and his ultimatum about going home. "No! No, of course not. I invited you here because I'm attracted to you. I…" She approached him and smiled while hoping she was projecting confidence and certainty. He remained still and watchful, and she closed the remaining distance between them to rest her hands against his chest. The heat coming off him, even through his cotton shirt, seared her fingers. Megan tipped her head back, so she could meet his eyes. "I don't do this…proposition a man, because I'm a public figure. You can't believe the trust involved because the public are fickle. If the public don't like me as a person, they're less likely to watch the show I work on, and I lose my approval rating. I value my reputation."

"I'm not forcing you to do anything."

95

Still testy. *Do something, Megan. Before he leaves.*

She kissed him.

It wasn't pretty. It wasn't polished. It wasn't even confident.

But her messy kiss got his attention.

He groaned, wrapped his arms around her so they plastered body to body and took over the kiss with a seductive ease that told her he'd done this before. He nibbled and licked and tempted. He enticed and cajoled, his hands shifted up and down her back, his fingers shaping and caressing her butt.

She gasped, desperate for air yet contrarily wanting the kiss to continue. He smelled so good and she wanted to wallow in the green and ginger scents that clung to his muscular body.

He lifted his head, his blue eyes glittering a weird color. She blinked, and when she glanced at him again, all she saw was sultry, seductive blue eyes. *Bedroom eyes.*

Jacey winked at her and rearranged his hands. Instead of copping a feel of her arse, he cupped her face and kissed her again. This time she was prepared for the jolt of heat, of pleasure and belonging that shot through her. He took the kiss deeper, using his tongue and lips to good effect. Megan pushed her body against his, reveling in the hard planes of muscle and his shaft pressing into her belly.

Her agent had been so wrong about a younger man.

What she needed, what she craved, was this man.

Jacey, who knew exactly what to do with her body to make it sing.

He pulled back a fraction, breaking their kiss. "What is

96

this between us, Megan?"

"Hot sex," she murmured. "Two adults indulging in pleasure."

"I want more," Jacey said, not taking his gaze off her.

"But you don't know me." She tingled, not pretending to misunderstand him.

Jacey ran his thumb over her top lip, his eyes doing that weird glitter thing again. "I want to know you."

"But I'm leaving here after the tournament."

"You told me you have a week off work. Stay here and spend time with me. You can stay with me. Henry and Gerard have given me a suite of rooms, so we'll have plenty of time to get to know each other. Privacy."

"Won't the locals gossip?"

"They won't speak to the press. Most of them, at any rate. And anyway, what would it matter? You're on holiday with a friend. People do it all the time."

"What happens after that?"

"Whatever we want. We'll remain friends or we won't. It depends how we fit together. We won't be any different from other couples getting to know each other," Jacey said, his voice patient. "But I want more than two nights."

"All right. I'll spend at least part of my holiday here. I can think about my future here as easily as I can in my apartment. Is that all?"

Jacey swept her off her feet with a suddenness that made her squeak. Without hesitation, he strode toward her bedroom. He dropped her on the king-size mattress and let his gaze wander her body. "Too many clothes."

"You could fix that."

"I could." He stooped to remove his black boots and let them thump to the floor one at a time. His socks dropped beside them. His big hands unfastened the buttons of his cream shirt, giving her tantalizing glimpses of his muscular chest.

Happiness slid through her as she watched him, and she followed her gut instincts to let this continue. "Don't you feel the cold? It is freezing outside."

Jacey shrugged his shoulders and the cotton shirt fluttered downward, leaving him standing in front of her in a pair of inky-blue jeans.

"How old are you?" she blurted, staring in shock at his abs. His wasn't the body of an older man. Yes, his hair had turned silver, but it was obvious he took care of himself.

"Older than you," he said with a wink and he prowled closer to the bed. He sat at the end and reached for her boots. One big hand took her foot by the ankle. The side zipper rasped downward with his tugging fingers. The black leather encasing her calves parted, and her pulse raced. He pulled the boot off her foot and dropped it on the floor before repeating the action with the other while she watched in amazement. No one took care of her in this way. She closed her eyes, swirling in a mass of excitement and nerves and a teenage urge to scream with acute anticipation.

Never had the removal of clothes seemed so sexy, and he hadn't even reached the good stuff.

He smoothed his fingers up her calf, his hands warm even through her socks. "Besides, age is only a number. You know that."

"Yes, you're right. I'll just stare at your muscles and appreciate them then."

"You get right on that," Jacey said with a smile. He slid off her bright pink-and-gray socks, then massaged the arches of her feet.

"Oh," she moaned. "I need this after an awards dinner when I have to get out the glad rags and my high heels." The man had skills.

Jacey set her feet on the mattress. He grinned at her as he crawled up the bed to straddle her hips. "Time for you to show skin."

Her heart skipped a beat as he lifted her jumper and tugged it over her head. Since her jumper was cashmere and wool and very warm, she'd worn a thin T-shirt with British Isles plastered on the front. The unveiling of her T-shirt seemed to amuse him. "Something funny?"

"I didn't expect a T-shirt."

"I like them. They're comfortable and don't crease—"

"You don't have to justify yourself, sweet pea. I wasn't criticizing."

The expression in his eyes...was that tenderness? Suddenly breathless, she stared at him, mesmerized by the heat, the other impossible emotions she was sure she was projecting on him rather than seeing herself. Despite considering Janet's advice, she'd never done many fast, short-term relationships. She preferred to get to know someone first before diving into greater intimacy. Old-fashioned perhaps, but her stance had saved her from embarrassment, and while reporters wrote about her love life, they didn't have photos or the leaked sex tapes that two of her male colleagues had racked up. But there was something about Jacey. Yes, she'd kissed his son, but she'd been aware of him, his enticing scent that made her woozy with delight and longing.

"You're frowning. What are you thinking?"

Megan pulled away from him and propped up the pillows so she could sit in comfort. "I don't do this...jump into bed with a man I don't know." She felt herself frown as her body ached for his touch, his possession. "But something about you makes me want to break my self-imposed rules. Jacey, tell me you're not playing me, that you won't sell a story to the press. I-I couldn't bear to learn that this...this connection I feel between us is nothing more than my imagination."

"You feel it too," he murmured, his eyes going bright blue then flaring with that strange light she'd noticed earlier. "I thought you did, but I wasn't sure."

"I feel as if you've bewitched me and stolen my commonsense. It scares me, makes me worry I'm moving too fast." Yeah, she didn't do short-term and casual because she craved a connection—the same connection she'd experienced with Charlie.

"Megan, you are safe with me. I would never betray you. You don't know me well enough to understand that yet, but we'll get there."

"You're talking about a future." What man did that? What woman believed him?

"I told you earlier this isn't casual for me, and I want more than two days."

Megan felt her forehead crinkle into a frown and hastily

smoothed it out. Lines had a way of settling in to stay these days. "I travel a lot for my job. Long distance relationships are hard. I've learned that before and have the scars to prove it."

"Shush, sweet pea. Let's go one day at a time and not worry about the hard stuff yet. I want to touch your beautiful body, run my lips over your hipbone, savor your sweetness. I want to push into your heat and drive us both crazy before we tumble into pleasure."

Wow. "Yes," Megan said, mesmerized by his husky tones, seduced by his words. If this were a mistake, then she'd go out with an extravaganza of sensual fireworks.

"Good."

She basked under his approval, studying his face, the faint stubble on his lean cheeks. She lifted her hips to allow him to tug down her jeans. Her lacy panties came away with the denim, but she offered no protest.

His chest rose and fell with his harsh sigh, and his big hands shook as he lifted the hem of her mint-green T-shirt. He whisked it over her head and dealt with her bra in a speedy move that left her gasping with the suddenness of it, his competence.

"Beautiful," he said, and it seemed to her he meant the sentiment. It wasn't an empty compliment to appease and guarantee her cooperation.

"Take off your jeans," she whispered. "Then we don't have to stop later. I have a packet of condoms in the bedside drawer." She pointed.

"I thought you didn't do casual," he said, suspicion weighting his words.

Heat flooded her cheeks, and she licked her lips, knowing she'd have to admit the truth. She'd come to Middlemarch intending to bag a young hottie. "I don't. I was upset when I left Auckland, and I was talking to a friend. She suggested a one-night stand with a younger man might make me feel better. I—"

"You tried to seduce Henry," Jacey snapped. "You would've used my son that way? To make yourself feel better about losing a job?"

"I know, and I intend to apologize to Henry when I can find a private moment. I've never done anything like that before. Besides, I was drunk—no, that's a bad excuse, even if it is the truth. I was drunk and feeling sorry for myself and I made a mistake, one I'm not proud of making. If it's any consolation, I will never repeat my actions. I've learned my lesson." *Oh, please don't let Jacey leave.* It would serve her right if he did.

"So if I had been the youngest, you would have kissed me?"

"Tried to kiss you," she corrected. "I told you I'm terrible at seduction. I made a real mess of it and embarrassed myself."

"I was jealous of my son," Jacey growled, and it was a growl.

Every muscle and tendon in her pulled tight, her eyes rounding at the growl still rattling in his chest. "I'm so sorry." She swallowed, half of her wanting to run, yet she suspected she wouldn't get far.

He pulled away, and she mourned the loss of contact, even if it was just his thigh against hers. He grabbed his shirt and covered his muscular splendor.

"What are you doing?" He was leaving. No, he couldn't leave. This wasn't fair. She wrapped her arms around herself to hide her nakedness.

Jacey sat on the corner of the bed, and never had a king-size bed felt so big and empty. He pulled on his socks and boots and stood. "I'm going home. If you want to spend the night, get dressed. Come with me."

Megan gasped. "But what about the press? They'll see me. They'll take photos and ask nosy questions."

"So what? I told you this isn't casual for me. I don't want casual. I want a relationship. They'll see us together at some stage. You'll have to deal with the publicity."

He wasn't joking, and his set expression cried a man set on his course. "Wait. Jacey, think about this. The photos. The publicity. It's not fun. People are cruel, and they...they gossip."

"I have just as much to lose as you. I value my privacy, but I'm willing to do this. If that doesn't tell you of my commitment to starting a relationship between us, then I don't know what will. Five minutes, Megan. Decide." And he strode from her bedroom without a backward glance.

Panic roared through her, leaving her weak and shuddering. He couldn't leave. He wouldn't. How could he understand the reality of the press? What man walked away from no-strings sex? What man insisted on a commitment? None. Not in her experience. So why did his ultimatum leave her feeling off-balance?

Before she knew it, she was off the bed and scrambling back into her clothes. She thrust her feet into her boots and breathless, charged after him. Had he gone? She hadn't heard the door and her hearing was good. Always had been. "Jacey, wait!"

"Bring the condoms," he said, and this time, she heard the door opening and the echoing slam.

CHAPTER SEVEN

JACEY STRODE TO HENRY'S SUV and climbed into the driver's side. His hands were shaking, his gut roiling, so great was his relief his bluff had worked. She was coming with him. At least, he thought she was, although he wasn't sure his idea was a good one. If the press became nosy and hung around Middlemarch...yeah, the other shifters would have reason to evict him from the community.

Seconds ticked past.

One. Two.

He started the engine.

His wolf whined, but Jacey maintained control, his gaze on the door of the cottage.

It flew open, and Megan stood in the light spilling from inside. She glanced in his direction, her boots unzipped, handbag looped over her arm, her coat on but unbuttoned against the cold.

She shivered and paused to zip her boots before she shut

the door and hurried to his vehicle. Jacey leaned over and opened the passenger door for her, and she started.

Her face was pale with two bright spots on her cheeks.

"Put on your seat belt."

She set her bag down and fumbled for the seat belt. The instant he heard the click of it sliding home, he took off.

In his peripheral vision, he saw the quick looks she flashed in his direction, felt the tension bleeding from him. She wasn't sure of him, yet she'd jumped and taken a risk on his sincerity. It meant a lot to Jacey, and he wouldn't forget her leap of faith.

They drove in silence, Jacey to keep control on his eager wolf and Megan...well, Megan was probably wondering if she'd hooked up with a madman. He drove past the café, closed now, but nothing appeared out of the ordinary. Not one reporter in sight. Just as he'd suspected.

They'd heard Megan's statement and had hurried off to their burrows to file their stories in comfort, out of the chilly breeze that forecast a colder spell.

A short drive later, he pulled up at Henry and Gerard's property. His home now since the boys had added a new suite of rooms just for him. There was a private entrance, but he didn't intend to use that one tonight.

He parked Henry's SUV in its usual place and turned to Megan. "Wait there."

She opened her mouth and closed it again, her features taking on an apprehensive cast.

Jacey sighed. She didn't get it, didn't understand yet, but he'd cut off his right arm before he hurt her. She was the one his wolf wanted, and he, the man, desired her more than he'd coveted another woman since Moira. Good enough for now.

He strode around the front of the vehicle and opened the door for her.

She stared at him for an instant before unclicking her seat belt and climbing from the vehicle, her handbag hitched over her arm. "Thank you," she murmured.

The lights were on, and he could hear the rumble of Henry's and Gerard's voices. The feminine laughter interspersing the masculine chatter brought satisfaction. Gerard deserved his happiness. It pleased him to see the man that felt like another son finding his mate. Now, he had to pray for Henry to heal and find someone to love. Wolves were lucky in that there was always a range of possibilities for mates. Once they took a mate, those possibilities ended until the death of one partner.

He was proof of that with the way his wolf kept insisting on Megan. After Moira died, he hadn't wanted another woman in the same way. Yeah, he'd started having sex again, but until Megan, he hadn't met a woman who offered the possibility of more.

"Come on." With long strides, he ushered her toward the main door, which led into the communal area of the house. The chatter in the room halted, and he knew his presence and perhaps Megan's had been noted. Geoffrey barked.

He opened the door and stood aside to let her enter. She hesitated, her face still pale, and he felt like a brute. His wolf growled and some of that angst bled free. Her eyes widened.

"Megan?"

She continued to stare.

"Have you changed your mind? I can take you home, and we won't see each other again."

"I brought the condoms," she blurted, and he grinned as a delightful shade of pink flooded her cheeks.

"Who brought condoms?" London whispered.

Gerard smirked, her prim English accent never failing to turn him on. God, he loved his English. He squeezed her knee and held a finger to his lips before he glanced at Henry. Geoffrey, Henry's Jack Russell, lifted his head from his basket and stared toward the hall.

His friend rolled his eyes, and Gerard wanted to cackle. He held back his amusement and paused the rugby game they were watching on the big screen TV. All three of them turned toward the entrance hall to await further information.

Instead of heading for his private quarters, or using his private entrance, Jacey directed his guest toward them.

"Henry," Jacey said, halting by the low table bearing a vase of white and pink roses. "You've met Megan."

Henry nodded. "The woman who drunk-kissed me."

Gerard heard London's gasp, her smothered laughter, but he was too busy watching the other players in this conversation to chuckle with his mate.

Henry remained impassive, but Gerard caught the slight tic in his jaw. Jacey attempted amused but Henry's words, or maybe it was the kiss, Gerard thought in enlightenment, made Jacey grind his teeth together. Megan Saxon went scarlet. Hmm, curious. Gerard turned his head to wink at London.

London broke the silence, humor dancing across her pale, freckled features. "Too much wine is a bad thing. I've learned that. You end up doing things you shouldn't, like joining in a zombie run. With obstacles. Big, fat, scary obstacles," she added with a theatrical shudder.

"How do you know it was wine?" Megan blurted.

"It's my drink of choice, but really, it was a guess. Alcohol in any form can make a person do stupid things," London said.

Megan took a huge shuddering breath and turned to Henry. "I'm very sorry I tried to kiss you. I embarrassed you, and I've embarrassed myself. It was obvious you weren't interested, but I kissed you anyway. I apologize. I promise to never do anything like that again."

A low growl attracted all their attention, and they turned to face Jacey. He froze, unaware the wolf had bled free until they stared at him. It said a lot about his feelings for Megan Saxon. This, and the fact that Jacey never brought women home, not when they'd been kids running around the Christchurch countryside or teenagers, at least not while he and Henry were around, made Gerard inspect Megan Saxon.

Blonde hair, trim figure, blue eyes. Above average height. Her commentating skills had impressed him before she'd arrived in Middlemarch, and her presence as a guest for the Sevens tournament had attracted the crowds and made the inaugural tournament a huge success. He bit his lip to halt his snort of laughter because her T-shirt was inside out beneath the blue woolen coat.

Megan took a deep breath and turned to Jacey. "Jacey, I want to apologize to you again too. I'm sorry you had to witness my stupid drunken behavior. Everything got on top of me and I behaved without considering the consequences."

Jacey gave a curt nod.

"Would you like a drink?" London raked her fingers through her long brown hair. "A glass of wine or a cup of tea? I was just going to make a pot of tea."

"No thank you, London," Jacey said. "Megan and I are off to bed."

Henry made a slight spluttering sound while Gerard allowed his amusement free in a loud chuckle.

"Pop, I'm glad you brought condoms with you," London said and even kept her face straight. She'd taken to calling Jacey Pop since he was Henry's father and like a father to Gerard too. London liked Jacey and enjoyed having him around. "Or rather, Megan did."

Her teasing told Gerard that, although he'd worried about their communal living arrangement, he didn't need to any longer. Three men capable of mowing lawns and dealing with yucky stuff like rubbish and tiny mice seeking warmth in the winter—she could deal, London had informed him.

"I believe in safe sex," Jacey replied. "We'll see you in the morning. It's my turn to cook breakfast. Don't be late." He guided a scarlet Megan past the brown leather couches where they sat, past the music sound system and heating controls on the wall and out of the communal living room.

There was a moment of heavy silence.

"You never told us that Megan Saxon kissed you. How was it?" London asked.

"She kissed my cheek," Henry corrected. "I wasn't going to let her kiss me when I knew Jacey was interested in her. Besides," he added gruffly. "She smelled wrong. She wasn't Jenny."

Gerard leaned back and wriggled to find a comfortable spot. "I've never seen him with that macho vibe."

"She pissed him off." Henry brushed back a lock of overlong dark blond hair. "You know he seldom loses his temper, but she's pushed his buttons and he's had enough."

London made a humming sound, her blue eyes dancing with mischief. "Interesting."

"Does it bother you seeing Jacey with another woman?" Gerard asked, deciding to confront that straight off.

"I've met some of the women Jacey has dated, but he's never brought them home, at least not while I've been there," Henry said. "It makes me think about my mother, but Jacey deserves happiness. I'd never begrudge him that."

"Well, at least they have condoms," London quipped. "We don't have to give him the safe-sex lecture."

Henry spluttered at her irreverence while Gerard shook his head in a sorrowful manner.

"What? You want a baby brother or sister?"

Henry's mouth fell open, and Gerard suspected he mirrored his best friend's visage.

"You do both know that sex produces babies? Those

SHELLEY MUNRO

rumors about storks and cabbage patches are wrong."

"Spank her," Henry said, but Gerard could tell his friend wasn't averse to having a baby brother, that the idea of a kid brother intrigued him. Henry wished Jacey happy.

Good enough. "I'm thinking breakfast might be interesting," Gerard said.

Henry met his gaze and agreed with a jerk of his chin.

"Me too," London said. "I wouldn't miss it for the world."

Megan followed Jacey, her cheeks burning with a fiery heat. Her hands fisted at her sides, anger burning through her in a cleansing wash. She...he...

Jacey halted and turned to her. On seeing her expression, he made a soft sound and held out his right hand.

A growl formed in her chest and it burned as it exited her throat. "You embarrassed me on purpose. You knew—"

"Knew that my son and his friends would tease you? It was a possibility," he conceded. "But they did nothing wrong. A little teasing never hurt. You started it by blurting out about the condoms."

"I didn't know anyone would hear," she cried. "I thought we were the only ones here."

"They would divulge nothing you said to the press or anyone outside this house." Jacey tugged on her hand and moved toward a wooden door. "This is my private suite of rooms. No one will overhear us. No one will disturb us. Gerard, Henry and I all have our own suites where we can be alone or entertain and we share the common rooms—the kitchen, the living room and the dining room."

"That's unusual."

"Maybe, but we get on well together and this is our home. I love the two boys and I enjoy London's company. Enough talk." He opened the door and pulled her inside.

Despite planting her weight on her booted feet, his strength popped her through the door like a cork coming free from a champagne bottle. She landed against his chest with a loud *oomph* as her breath whooshed free.

Jacey shut the door and flipped the lock.

Megan shot him a look of panic. He had locked the door. What did he intend to do to her?

"The lock opens from the inside without a key. You can leave. I'm not forcing you to stay."

Megan swallowed, so off-balance she just stared at him, her pulse racing as if she'd run a hundred-meter sprint. She didn't know what she was doing or why she was doing it, yet she felt compelled somehow. Not that he was forcing her, but it was something deep-seated inside her, a small voice that whispered if she didn't see where this relationship with Jacey went, she'd regret it for the rest of her days.

Swallowing for what felt like the *nth* time, she glanced down and froze. Her handbag dropped with a thud. "Why didn't you tell me my T-shirt was inside out?"

"I didn't notice until we arrived here." Jacey closed the distance between them and before she could blink, he'd tugged off her coat and tossed it aside. Seconds later, she no longer wore a T-shirt, and instinctively, she crossed her

113

hands over her naked breasts.

She hadn't taken the time to put on a bra, but had stuffed fresh underwear into her handbag along with her toothbrush.

Jacey tugged her toward the bed. "Jeans off," he ordered.

She frowned at his back as he turned away to switch on a bedside lamp. Now that she could see better, she studied the room with interest. A big king-size bed, the décor masculine in shades of brown and cream. Off to the right there was a small lounge area with a two-seater and a flat-screen television. Beyond the two-seater was a sliding door leading outside. With the curtains still open, she could see darkness only—not a single house light or streetlamp. Another wall held a bookcase stuffed full of books of all shapes and sizes. Off to the left, there was another door.

"The bathroom," Jacey said, noticing her glance. "You're still wearing your jeans."

She shivered at the note of authority. It wasn't fear. It was something else, an urge to obey him and a fascination at the way he'd changed from amiable companion to demanding lover.

Her hands went to the waistband of her jeans before her brain issued the command. She wriggled from the tight denim, then realized she still wore her boots.

"Let me," Jacey said, and she saw he was already naked and *very* ready for the next step. "Sit on the bed."

She obeyed in silence and watched his bent head as he lifted her left foot, unzipped her boot and removed it. He said nothing about her lack of socks, but removed the boot from her right foot and helped her to stand.

Megan removed her jeans and her lacy panties.

"I thought you were beautiful the first time I saw you," he murmured.

Then, with another one of those lightning-fast moves, he scooped her off her feet and dropped her in the middle of the bed. He caged her between his hard body and the mattress, his lips on hers cutting off any chance of speech. He devoured her. There was no other word for it. Her mind blanked as his lips ravished hers, his hands roving her shoulders, her collarbone, her hips and her buttocks.

Rocked to her core by his passion and her own response, she gripped his brawny shoulders and held tight, kissing him back, exploring his back and the warmth of him. Heat radiated from him, and it felt as if she were on fire inside and out.

He trailed kisses down her neck and nibbled at the point where her shoulder and neck met. Sparks of pleasure shot to her toes, the nibbles turning to sucking and biting.

"Jacey," she murmured against his neck, unsure of what she was asking for. She ran her hand down his broad back and lower to his muscular butt. Jacey thrust his thigh between hers and pressed it against her mound. A low-level simmer sprang to life in her belly, and she moaned, greedy for more.

"Megan," he whispered.

Eyes she didn't remember shutting flicked open. In the faint light of the one lamp, his face looked tense and stonelike, but his eyes...his eyes glowed with the strange flare of color—a tawny amber that she'd decided was her imagination. Now she wasn't so sure. Freaky. A little scary, but she was right where she wanted to be.

"Megan?"

"Yes?" She met that blue and tawny-amber gaze without flinching.

Her reply seemed to reassure him, and he parted their bodies, rearranging them before he kissed her again. Slow. Drugging. Fast. Fleeting. His hand shaped one breast, and he gave the nipple a sharp tug. The shard of pain rocked straight to her sex, the low-level arousal ramping up another notch.

She moaned, arching her body in a silent demand for more. She'd always enjoyed a little roughness, but most of her past lovers had hesitated to hurt her. Not that Jacey was hurting her. It was more an edge to his touch.

"I have to taste you," he said. "Your scent is driving me crazy."

He moved away from her again, roughly parted her legs and lifted her to his mouth.

Oh. *Oh!* His tongue. It was rough and aggressive and licked down the seam of her folds. His tongue traced a rough circle around her entrance, gathering her juices.

"Nice." The husky word vibrated against her flesh, skimming toward her needy clit. He slid a finger inside her, testing her readiness. It thrust inside her, firing nerve endings, yet not giving her enough. His mouth dragged upward toward her clit. He tongued her with a firm touch.

"Jacey." His name was a plea, and her hands, which had found their way into his hair, gripped and tugged, urging him to give her more.

He teased her nub with perfect pressure and filled her with another finger, dragging his digits in and out of her channel in time with the laps and massage of his tongue. She flew up, the pleasure like a rollicking crescendo. She scaled the peak with a sharp jolt of sensation speeding to her toes, then shuddered with rhythmic pulses clutching his two fingers.

Once her breathing dropped to normal, he moved up the bed and kissed her. This was a slow kiss, one of passion that set her senses leaping to life. She tasted herself on his lips, recognized the scent of arousal.

"Okay?"

"Very okay," she whispered.

He reached past her and pulled out a condom. She stared at the foil packet in his hand, stared as he ripped it open, stared as he rolled it onto his shaft.

"You had condoms," she said, and her voice held accusation.

"I do," he said as he rearranged her body and parted her legs. He fitted himself to her and pushed inside, taking it slow and easy when she wasn't sure what to expect.

"Why did you tell me to bring my packet?"

He met her gaze and pulled back, his eyes glowing with that weird light yet again. It seemed to appear whenever he became aroused. "Because I didn't want to run out." He pushed deep this time, and although it wasn't painful, her body struggled to adjust to him.

He didn't want to run out of condoms? How long was he intending to keep her in this room? He had said they would meet for breakfast. Yes, he had said that.

"You feel like silk around me. So much better than my imagination."

He pulled back and plunged home. Heat sizzled to life in her, and she slipped her hand between their straining bodies. She never came like this, not without additional stimulation, and she wasn't about to miss out because of his lack of knowledge of her body.

"Good girl," he said, surprising her. "Take what you want."

He increased the speed of his thrusts, his features hard and a little scary. He kissed her lips, her neck and sucked hard. The shot of pain did it for her. She gasped and rubbed her clit, the orgasm rolling through her again in a powerful wave. Her pussy rippled around his length and he sucked another mark, on her breast this time. He stroked harder. Faster. Faster. *Faster*. Without warning, he stilled, a groan rippling from his throat—a hoarse sound of enjoyment.

What seemed like a long time later, he pulled out and removed the condom.

He drew back the covers, lifted her effortlessly and joined her in the bed. He switched off the lamp, plunging the room into darkness before curling his body around hers. She thought about their lovemaking, and it had been lovemaking because it was a step above normal sex. The man had done it for her.

Twice. Way to end her drought.

Megan dozed off, satisfied and relaxed after the stupendous sex. She woke what must've been hours later because the room was much lighter. Jacey nuzzled her neck, pressing her back to his chest.

"Lift your leg," he murmured and adjusted her position to his satisfaction. His hand slipped between her legs, teased her flesh and heat punched her. He moved his hand, and she moaned in disappointment.

"Jacey."

"Shush, sweet pea. Don't move." He shifted his hips, and she felt the prod of his cock. With his hand, he maneuvered into position and seconds later, he filled her aching pussy. In this position she couldn't move, couldn't reposition but he did all the work with his cock and his talented fingers. This climax was slow building, going up, up, up until she thought she might scream her frustration. He slid deep, rocking his hips and alternatively flicking and teasing her clit with a slow pass of his thumb. He kissed her neck, suction coming into play. The slight prick of a sharp tooth sent her into orbit.

Megan groaned and let him move her limp body into another position. On her hands and knees, he thrust into her from behind, his cock surging deep and hard. Megan groaned a second time, the tiny spasm fluttering to life again.

The growl coming from Jacey didn't even seem strange because she wanted to growl and roar with the pleasure of this joining too. He collapsed against her back and she bore his weight without complaint.

"Each time is better," he murmured against her ear.

And she had to agree. "Yes."

He pressed a kiss to her neck and pulled free. She heard the snap of latex as she crawled beneath the covers again. Good grief. She hadn't even registered the need for a condom, which told her everything. This man had sneaked beneath her defenses without even breaking a sweat. Yes, they'd argued, had a disagreement or whatever the classification for what they had was. Was this make-up sex? She'd have to think about it later once she was alone.

Jacey cuddled in beside her and the last thing she remembered was thinking about how nice and cozy it was with two people in the bed.

CHAPTER EIGHT

LONDON STUDIED THE KITCHEN clock and watched it click over to seven-thirty. She tied an apron around her waist and pondered a diet for all of two seconds. Nah. Gerard loved her curvy frame. "Maybe I'll start breakfast. Scrambled eggs and bacon?"

Henry sipped his black coffee, gaze on the clock. "Interesting."

"Isn't it?" Gerard agreed, closing one pale green eye in a wink.

"Don't tease Jacey," London ordered.

Henry and Gerard exchanged a glance, and London didn't have to be a mind reader to know where their thoughts headed.

"You'll embarrass Megan. She might do a runner."

"English, you mortified her enough last night with your condom questions."

A sliver of guilt pierced London. She bit her lip as she

reached for a carton of eggs. "I know. I couldn't help it. Pop didn't react though, apart from his eyes. When he's emotional, they shift a little wolfish. Yours don't. Not that I've noticed," she said over her shoulder to Henry.

With efficient moves, she cracked a dozen eggs into a bowl. She added milk, salt and pepper and whisked them together.

"Megan will need clothes, otherwise she'll be late for the game. I think she'll fit the clothes hanging in our wardrobe, the ones at the far end. Gerard, can you grab a couple of matching outfits and deliver them to Jacey's suite?"

Henry slid off his stool at the breakfast counter. "I'll give them a wake-up call."

Geoffrey rose from his basket to follow him.

"Aw." Gerard sounded like a small boy. "I wanted to wake them. Don't do it until I get there with the clothes."

The two men and Geoffrey hastened from the kitchen.

Jenny's clothes—ones she hadn't had the heart to throw away, not that she'd mentioned it to Henry. It would be good for someone to get use out of them. London put the bacon under the grill and pulled out the bread to make toast, all while keeping an eye on the eggs she'd started to cook.

Henry and Gerard arrived back in the kitchen together, their mischievous expressions making her groan. "You teased them."

"Couldn't let the opportunity pass," Henry confirmed in a gruff voice.

Gerard's eyes danced with humor. "Geoffrey pushed through the door and darted into the suite. We had to get him."

"What happened?" Her curiosity got the better of London.

"Megan opened the door, wearing Jacey's shirt. Jacey was in the shower. There were clothes all over the floor." Henry's expression slid close to a smile, closer than London had seen in months.

"Why is that funny?"

"Jacey used to lecture us about everything having a place, and it wasn't the floor. We had to pick up clothes and things, or we'd end up chopping wood or doing some other chore," Gerard explained. "I've a good mind to get our ax and present it to him when he shows his face."

"Did you embarrass Megan?"

"No," Gerard said.

"Yes," Henry countered. "Although she was very polite and thanked us for the clothes. She goes bright red—the same color she went last night."

Both men sniggered and Geoffrey barked.

"You two are behaving like teenagers," London chided. "Can one of you get the plates and set the table? We'll need another pot of coffee too." She scooped up four slices of toast and popped four more into the toaster.

Geoffrey barked, and London turned to see Jacey lead Megan into the kitchen.

"I'm sorry we're late. London, thank you for cooking. I'll take your next turn," Jacey said.

London clapped her hands together. "Megan, you look great. That red suits you."

"Thanks," Megan murmured, and she had trouble

meeting any of their gazes.

London noticed the bruises—good, old-fashioned hickeys on her neck. "I have a scarf that will go with your outfit. I'll get it for you before you leave for the Sevens tournament."

"Thanks."

Jacey ushered Megan to the table and into the seat next to his usual position. Henry organized the new pot of coffee while Gerard hustled to set the table.

"We weren't late to breakfast, Pop," London said as she placed a platter of eggs and bacon on the middle of the table. Oh, she was terrible. Just as bad as Gerard and Henry.

Henry and Gerard sniggered again, and London rolled her eyes. Juveniles. Although they were right about one thing—Megan turned a delightful shade of red.

"Big mosquitoes in your room last night, Jacey." Gerard's lips quivered. "Do we need to call a pest control company?"

"Enough," Jacey barked, his patience with their teasing at an end. "Let us eat our breakfast in peace. Megan will be staying tonight."

Megan winced and finally looked up from the piece of toast Jacey had foisted on her. "Oh, but—"

"You will stay here." Jacey covered her hand with his to snare her attention. "Please, I want you to stay here."

London felt as if she were in the middle of a rom-com movie and wanted to sigh. Jacey wanted Megan. That much was obvious to her now that she knew more about shifters. Megan wanted Jacey too, but she was fighting the pull between them. "Coffee, Megan? Jacey?"

"Please," Jacey said, offering her a grateful look.

Henry stood. "I'll get it."

"Megan, do you have a guess as to which team will win the cup today?"

"I think the local team is in with a good chance. The players seem to have an innate instinct of where the opposition will go and are a close-knit team," she said, gaining confidence as she spoke. "I'd be surprised if they don't win. If not, they'll certainly make the final."

"Did you really play rugby for New Zealand?" London asked.

"It seems like a long time ago now, but yes. The women's team. We won the World Championship for the three years I played."

Interest burned in London. "Why did you stop playing?"

"I hurt my knee. It healed, but it was never as strong. If I do too much walking or running on it now, it aches."

"What time do you need to be at the school?" Jacey asked.

Megan glanced at her watch and gasped. "In half an hour."

Jacey patted her hand, then lifted it and placed it on his lap. "Do you have everything you need to get ready?"

Her brow furrowed. "I have an emergency makeup kit in my handbag, and thanks to London, I look professional."

"You're staying here tonight," Jacey said. "We can pick up your stuff and check out of your cottage later tonight, or if you're busy, I can do it for you."

"No!" Megan said. Unfortunately, too sharp and abrupt because Jacey scowled while Henry, Gerard and London had varying reactions, reactions she feared to decipher. "I don't need you organizing me." Her gaze jerked away and hit the dog. It seemed even he had an opinion because he chose that second to bark.

"Have you finished your breakfast?"

Megan dropped her gaze to her plate. She'd done nothing except gnaw the corner off a bit of toast and stir her spoonful of scrambled eggs around her plate. This was like no morning-after she'd ever experienced. "Yes."

"Good. We'll discuss this elsewhere."

Before she could blink, Jacey was guiding her toward his rooms. She let him shunt her inside, cringing at the oppressive silence. The door clicked behind them.

"We discussed this and agreed. I don't intend to be your dirty secret. I want the chance at a relationship with you, Megan. Things might not work out between us. I hope they do, but I want to give us a chance. That means not hiding. We're upfront with each other and say what we're thinking. Neither of us is young. We've both had other relationships and come with baggage. I get that my actions might seem pushy but I know what I want. I thought you wanted the same thing."

Her breath whooshed in, whooshed out. She stared at him, her throat tight. He overwhelmed her with his honesty, but how was she to know if it was an act?

"I'd better put on makeup," she said finally. "No, I'm

not trying to avoid the conversation, but I'm so confused. Jacey, you've blindsided me. I wasn't expecting this. You. I need to think."

"I've found too much thinking leads to problems," he muttered.

A laugh rippled from her, easing the strain in the room. "All right," she capitulated. "We'll pick up my stuff once I'm finished for the day."

"And you'll spend the rest of your holiday with me."

"Yes, if you don't mind seeing me in the same clothes."

"We can go shopping in Dunedin. Clothes are the easy part. London gave you two outfits."

"She did, which was nice of her. Okay, let me put on my makeup, otherwise I'll be late and that's not professional."

"I'll be in the kitchen. We can leave as soon as you're ready."

"Thanks." Megan closed the distance between them and stood on tiptoe to kiss his cheek.

"We can do better than that."

His arms came around her and her heart soared with expectation. The man kissed like no one else. He consumed her, drowning her in passion and excitement, making her feel as if she were the only woman in the world for him. He made her crave him, want more. And then there was his scent. Never had a scent seduced her but his...ah, she wanted to wallow in the decadence of it.

Jacey broke off the kiss. "Makeup," he said in a husky voice. "Not that you need it, but I know how women feel about these things."

He left her alone, and dazed, she placed her fingers on

her swollen lips. For the sex alone she would stay with him, but it was more. Something about this man made her want to be the woman he saw.

"Pop."

London saw him first and a rush of pleasure filled him on hearing *Pop*. Henry had always called him Jacey, although sometimes in moments of emotional crisis, he called him Dad. Jacey was okay with that because he knew Henry returned his love and respect. Gerard had followed Henry's lead and called him Jacey from their first meeting.

"Dad," Henry chided.

Jacey grinned, blinked back sudden emotion. "What?"

"You were rough on her," Gerard said.

Jacey glanced toward his suite and lowered his voice. "She's mate material. I want her to know I'm there for her, and I need to be blunt to cut through the emotional baggage in her past. The older we get, the more our memories and experiences color our actions."

"But you're going to give her romance too, Pop? We women like a little romance."

"Is that the same as hot sex?" Gerard asked and let out an *oomph* when London caught him in the ribs with her elbow.

Jacey laughed aloud since his mind had gone the same direction. "Don't worry. I've learned a thing or two over the years."

"Good to hear." London nodded with approval.

"I'm not sure I want to hear," Henry said, but he

appeared calm and relaxed, unworried about a woman entering Jacey's life.

"You approve?" Jacey asked.

"I've said it before," Henry replied. "She smells right, and I like her."

Gerard sniffed the air. "Your scents are entwined now."

"Yeah," Jacey said with satisfaction.

"What scent?" London demanded. "I can't smell a thing."

"Orange blossom with a hint of cinnamon and a green outdoors scent." The combination made him want to grin like a dope.

Henry sniffed too. "You've got a whole orchard thing going on."

"Yeah, great, isn't it?" Jacey said.

"If Megan is going to stay for a while, tell her I have plenty of clothes." London glanced at Henry and squared her shoulders. "They belonged to Jenny, and I couldn't bear to throw them away, so I kept them. I'll air them out, and if it's all right with you, I'll hang them in your suite wardrobe."

Jacey glanced at Henry, too, and found his son nodding. "That would be wonderful. I thought I might take Megan to Tekapo or maybe to Queenstown or in that direction for a few days. Do you have warm clothes?"

"Yes." She cleared her throat. "It will be good to see someone wearing them. It will bring back the fun memories. Is that okay, Henry?"

"Yes," his son said, his eyes bright as if he held his emotions at bay with difficulty. "You're a good person,

London."

Jacey heard Megan shut the door of his suite and walk toward him. His wolf perked up, eager to spend time with his mate. He turned to watch her stride into the room, and the way her steps slowed when she realized they were all watching her appearance. Including Geoffrey who barked.

"Wow." London broke the silence. "Show me how you did your makeup. I can see you're wearing stuff but you were so quick, and it looks gorgeous. Natural and subtle, yet stunning."

"Thanks. I've learned a thing or two from the makeup department over the years. I'd be happy to show you."

"Megan, are you ready to go?" Jacey wanted to tell her she looked beautiful, but he'd conducted this romance in front of the kids enough already. He'd save his compliments for when they were alone. "Will we see you at the tournament?"

"Let me see," London said. "Watching sexy men run around the rugby field versus housework. Sexy men. Housework." She chortled at Gerard's growl. "I'll run and get you that scarf. You don't want to encourage questions."

Henry's pointed gaze shot to Megan's neck then back at him.

The boy was close to laughing and not spending so much time in his head. His friends were good for him. He and Megan were helping in the entertainment department too. Jacey smiled. The things he did for his son, although he'd be careful about marking Megan in future. He had thought little last night in his urgency to touch her. He wouldn't make the same mistake again because he didn't want to embarrass her in public and cause a storm of gossip.

Outside, he opened the passenger door for Megan and waited for her to seat herself before he closed it. Whistling, he jogged around the rear of the vehicle and slid into the driver's seat. He shot a glance at her, everything inside him clenching.

She draped the scarf around her neck with practiced ease. "Does that work?"

"You look beautiful. I've been remiss not telling you earlier. Red suits you."

"Thanks."

He started the vehicle. "Now is the time to tell me if I'm coercing you into going against your wishes."

"No." She let out a sigh. "I want to know you better. It's the suddenness and...well, yes. I want to spend time with you."

"Good." His mind filled in what she didn't say. Something about the rawness and intense nature of what was between them. Another wolf would understand. He hoped it was her instincts trying to tell her he was a good prospective mate. "Are your family in New Zealand?"

It wouldn't hurt to learn about her background, to work out the origins of her wolfish scent. While a werewolf could have offspring with a human, the wolf line became diluted, and they lost the power to shift. He suspected a wolf or two lurked in Megan's ancestral tree rather than a scent transference from another wolf with whom she'd crossed paths. If it was transference, a shower would lessen the scent, but it remained at the same strength.

"My parents are off on a world cruise. They travel a lot and my sister and I have trouble keeping up with them. Tessa talked to them a few days ago, and they said they were heading home so they could be here when my sister gives birth. Her second child is due soon."

"Are you going to spend time with your sister?"

"I'll try, but it depends on work. We keep in contact via email and skype. While I'm not always physically present, I don't miss out on much."

"You're close."

"Yes. There is five years between us, but we are close. Closer now than we were when we were kids. What about you?"

"I was adopted," Jacey replied. "My adoptive parents were great. I had a happy childhood. They died several years ago. There is just Henry and me now. Were your parents born in New Zealand?"

"Why?"

"There is a faint accent to some of your words. I wasn't sure if it is because you travel a lot or because your parents didn't come from New Zealand."

"Huh. Most people don't pick up on that. My mother is Swiss and my father is Scottish. They moved to New Zealand before Tessa and I were born."

Interesting. Both places had or were near wolf populations. Forty years ago or longer, certainly. He could research himself or maybe ask London. She was a whiz with computer research and would be much quicker than him.

He pulled into the school car park, and at once reporters surrounded his vehicle.

"Perfect," Megan bit out.

"You don't have to tell them anything," Jacey said.

She sucked in a breath, nodded.

"Let me open the door for you, so I can keep them away."

"Thank you. I'd appreciate that."

"Mr. Anderson. Mr. Anderson. What is your relationship with Megan?" a reporter shouted.

Quick work on their part, ferreting out his name. He ignored the shouts and rounded the vehicle to open the door for Megan.

"Megan, is Jacey Anderson your new boyfriend?"

"Good morning," Megan said in a bright voice. "I'm looking forward to the final day of the Kenneth Nesbitt Sevens tournament. There are some skilled teams and the rugby should be excellent. Don't miss it."

Approval filled Jacey.

"Megan. Megan!"

"Excuse me, boys. They can't start without the commentator."

Jacey pushed his way through the determined pack, taking his cue from Megan and ignoring their questions. They were like a pack of yipping dogs following along, shouting out nosy questions about their relationship. His wolf's hackles rose and the beginnings of a fierce growl rolled through his mind. None of their business.

Saber opened the door to the room the council had claimed for administration purposes and strode toward them with ground-eating steps. He pushed past the reporters, a fierce scowl fixed on his face. "Stand back," he warned. "Please allow our commentator through."

With Saber's help, he and Megan entered the relative peacefulness of the administration room, closing the door on the yapping reporters.

"Wow," Agnes, one of the feline elders on the council said in a stern tone. "We didn't expect your presence to bring such interest. Gate sales are way up for today, and the businesses nearby the school offering parking are raking in cash."

"Good," Megan quipped. "Then you'll be able to afford to pay for me."

Agnes tsked. "Oh dear. I thought you knew. The network donated your services for the weekend."

"They did?" Megan asked. "That's unusual. They normally charge for this sort of thing."

"Contacts in high places," Agnes said and tapped her nose.

Jacey turned to Megan. "Will you be okay? I have a few things I need to do."

"We'll make sure no one bothers her," Saber said.

A slight man wearing spectacles pushed through a different door, one that led onto the playing fields. "We're just about ready to go. Where is—oh, there you are. We need to wire you for sound."

"I'm ready." Megan turned to Jacey, her manner becoming diffident. "Will you...are you coming back later?"

"I'll be here for the final and will drive you home

afterward. Okay?"

"Yes. Thank you."

Jacey wanted to kiss her goodbye, but not in front of Saber, Agnes and the soundman. He made do with reaching for her hand and giving it a quick squeeze. "See you later."

Showtime. The first game of the quarterfinals passed quickly, and Megan found herself immersed in the rugby, totally focused to match names with numbered jerseys. Between plays, she told short stories, commented on the players and the action on the field. Sometimes, she made things up or signaled for music to celebrate a try.

The soundman had pinned a mic to her borrowed jacket, and this allowed her to keep her hands free when she forgot a name and needed a quick refresher. Much easier with only seven players per team on the field at one time.

Over to her right, the temporary grandstand was full of people of all ages. The promised rain hadn't arrived and a fickle sun peeped from behind heavy clouds. "Looks as if the breeze will be with the Middlemarch Panthers for the second half. Middlemarch's kickoff, taken by Joe Mitchell. It's going up. The Middlemarch team is chasing, but number three of the Hyde Runners has the ball. Tackled by Saul Sinclair. The Hyde player has dropped the ball in the tackle. This Middlemarch team is fast, people. Look at Sly Mitchell go. He's passing to Felix Mitchell. Try!"

Before she knew it, the referee was glancing at his watch and blowing the final whistle.

"That's it for this game," Megan said. "The home team are through to the semi-finals. We have a ten-minute break before the next quarterfinal between the Dunedin Flyers and the Nelson Eagles kicks off. Don't go away, folks. We'll be back soon." Megan flicked off her mic and strode from the sideline toward the admin room.

A bunch of kids raced to her side, holding out pens and programs. She stopped to chat and autographed the programs for both boys and girls.

"I want to be a referee," one of the little girls said.

"Sylvie Mitchell," a blond boy scoffed. "Girls can't be referees."

"I can so," Sylvie said. "Daddy said I can be anything." She turned big brown eyes in Megan's direction. "I can be a referee."

Megan bit back a smile and nodded. "Of course you can. New Zealand has some top women referees. Here comes your father now."

The dark-haired girl glanced in the direction. "That's not Daddy. That's Uncle Saber. My daddy is Felix. He's playing for the Panthers. See," she said to the blond boy. "I can be a referee."

"Emily sent me to get you. She brought coffee and refreshments," Saber said.

"That would be great. I slept in and missed breakfast. Are the press people still hanging around?"

"Afraid so. There are three heading our direction right now. Let's hustle." Saber moved between her and the determined men jogging toward them.

"I'm sorry."

"Don't be. You're doing a brilliant job and the crowd is enjoying themselves. We're also making a killing at the gate. The local business owners are happy too, including Emily." Saber opened the door to the admin building and ushered her inside. He closed it firmly on the two reporters and one cameraman who had followed them across the field.

"Coffee or water?" Emily asked. "Or both?"

"Both please." Megan shrugged out of her black jacket to reveal the clinging red merino jumper beneath and her black trousers. "It got hot running up and down the field. I thought I might interview some of the players plus the referee at the end of the next match. Get their perspectives. What do you think?" she asked Saber and Agnes.

Agnes tapped her pen against her paper where she was keeping a list of the scores and the players on each team. "The crowd would enjoy that."

"That's a great idea," Saber said. "I'll allocate two men to keep the reporters away. I'll tell them to keep to the background unless they're needed."

"Thank you."

"Want a sandwich?" Emily asked. "Or would you prefer fruit?"

Megan's stomach gurgled. "Have I got time for half a sandwich?"

Agnes consulted her watch. "Five more minutes until kickoff."

Megan accepted the sandwich—ham and mustard—and practically inhaled it. "I'll take the water with me." She picked up her coffee and took a few sips while listening to Emily and Saber chatter about the games.

Agnes tapped her watch, her expression stern. "Time to get moving."

"The lunch break is half an hour," Emily said. "Should I bring more sandwiches?"

"Please." Megan scooped up her water and headed for the door.

The reporters were waiting for her.

"Megan! Megan, who is the man? Is he your lover?" one shouted.

Megan ignored the questions. "I am here to commentate the games. Kickoff is in one minute."

"What about Rowena? Is it true that the two of you are at war?"

"No, of course not," Megan said, shocked.

"Gentlemen, please let Ms. Saxon through. We are ready to start the next game," Saber said in a no-nonsense voice.

Thankfully, they took a collective step back and allowed her to pass. She flicked on her microphone and got back to work.

Chapter Nine

"Any ideas where I should take Megan for a couple of days' break?" Jacey directed his question to Gerard and Henry as they worked together on a quote for a new job in Queenstown.

Gerard lifted his gaze from his laptop. "Wanaka is nice."

"No, stay away from the touristy areas. More chance of someone recognizing Megan," Henry said. "What about Cromwell? It's an interesting town because of the way they flooded the old town to create the dam. There are good pubs—historical ones. You can check out the old gold mining sites and there are loads of vineyards to visit. You could play golf or go for a walk. Book in at a motel or one of the upmarket places that will guarantee your privacy."

"Good suggestion." Gerard nodded approval. "Make sure you wear hats and sunglasses when you go out in public. Henry is right. Cromwell would be perfect—low-key and relaxing. Reporters would expect

139

you to go to Queenstown or Wanaka or farther afield."

"Plan," Jacey said.

"Pop." Gerard surprised Jacey until he deciphered the teasing in the young man. "This role reversal is kind of fun. Now I know you're using condoms, but do you need any other advice?" Gerard stood to drape his arm around Henry's broad shoulders, and his son and best friend studied him, eyes ablaze with their pleasure at the teasing. "Henry and I would be glad to offer our help. What are you wearing?"

A snort erupted from Jacey. "As little as possible, and that's all you need to know, pups. I can handle things from here without your help. I'm not too old to manage internet research. What else do we need to consider for the quote? Extra labor? Where are you going to find more labor out here?"

"Not a problem," Henry said. "I spoke to Joe and Sly Mitchell yesterday between games. The twins are looking for work now that they've almost finished at varsity. Joe told me they have their eye on a parcel of land and want to save a deposit. He said some of their friends would lend a hand."

"Good." Gerard sat in front of his laptop again. "Leo suggested I check in with his brothers. He said that he and Isabella would help us in a jam. Felix and Saber too, although they need more notice to juggle their other responsibilities."

Two hours later, Jacey drove back to the Middlemarch School, confident his plans were underway. Now all he had to do was sneak Megan out from under the noses of the reporters.

Cars jammed the area around the school, and he ended up parking by the café and walking back to the school.

"There he is!" someone shouted as he approached the entrance to the sports fields.

Jacey blinked as a man thrust a microphone at him.

"You! Sir? How long have you known Megan Saxon? Are you an item? How long have you been dating? Did you break up her relationship with the politician?"

What politician? Jacey frowned and ignored the questions to push past the growing crowd. Good grief. He should have waited for Henry and Gerard, but he'd been too impatient to see Megan again. Kind of funny—needing security when he was in the business.

"Do you live in Middlemarch?" a female reporter asked. She pressed closer and fluttered her eyelashes. "No one seems to know much about you. No one will talk to us."

Good. Jacey stepped around her and paid five dollars to enter the grounds. He scanned the three fields, his wolf eager to find Megan. He spotted her running up and down the sideline, her blonde hair streaming out behind her as she increased her pace to keep up with the play.

The referee checked his watch and blew his whistle, one team jumping and shouting with joy while their opposition hunched their shoulders in defeat. Only two points in the game.

Jacey approached Megan in long strides and, unable to help himself, drew her close for a quick kiss. His lips grazed her cheek and her scent, heightened by her recent exercise, cut him off at the knees. He grasped her shoulders to kiss her.

"Not here," Megan whispered.

He seized her hand and dragged her toward the admin building.

Several youngsters approached them, but something in his demeanor chased them away. Spying a gap between the admin building and the one next door, he dragged her into the privacy. Seconds later, his mouth was on hers, his hunger for her touch desperate, as if he hadn't seen her for weeks and days instead of mere hours. God, her touch, her scent, her sweet kisses. He couldn't get enough of her. Last night...not nearly enough.

When he lifted his head, she looked well kissed, and he took pride in the fact. He smoothed his fingers over her cheek, taking pleasure in the silky skin. *His.*

"I've arranged a few days away," he murmured. He stiffened as his words seemed to echo around them.

Megan's eyes went wide as she fumbled with the mic attached to her red jumper. A few sharp taps echoed as she fumbled to switch off the mic. "I think it's off now. I'm so sorry."

"Could have been worse," he said, pausing and smiling when there was no echo of his own voice around the sports ground. "I might have said that I can't wait to fuck you and feel your heat around my cock."

Megan spluttered out a laugh. "I might have said I can't wait to stroke that big boy again. Sorry. I'm normally more professional and never forget stuff like pesky microphones."

"No harm done," Jacey said. "At least I didn't blurt out

what my plans were for the next week. We can still sneak away before the reporters discover our destination."

"Are you going to tell me?"

"Trust me?"

Her instant nod brought a flush of pleasure in Jacey.

Somewhere nearby, a door opened. Jacey caught the swish of fabric. He turned and placed his body in front of Megan's.

"That was entertaining," Agnes said with a grimace. "Too bad for the reporters you realized before you mentioned anything incriminating. Are you doing the final from the sideline or from the commentary box?"

"The commentary box," Megan said. "The game will be fast, and I want to keep up."

Agnes nodded. "Emily delivered sandwiches and a flask of coffee for you." She took one step toward the admin building.

"Don't want you too exhausted for tonight," Jacey murmured.

"I heard that young man," Agnes said in a strident voice. She wagged her finger. "No more of these whispered confidences until you're away from the school. Innocent ears and all that."

"Yes, ma'am." Jacey struggled to keep a straight face.

Agnes shook her finger again. "Scallywag wolf," she muttered and closed the door behind her.

"What did she call you?"

"A scallywag," Jacey replied. "Come on. You need food. I saw you sprinting up and down the field."

"It was fun. The entire tournament has been fun."

"Better than you thought it would be." Jacey filled in the blanks.

"My boss foisted the job on me. Jeremy acted like it was a favor but the truth is they intended to send a junior reporter. The idea of visiting the country didn't enthuse me. It goes to show, I should never make snap judgments."

"I, for one, am glad you came to Middlemarch." Jacey guided her toward the admin building and opened the door for her.

"That was entertaining." Saber glanced up from his laptop and the spreadsheet he was working on with the scores and individual scoring statistics.

Jacey took a bow. "Thank you. Thank you very much."

"What we've done is fuel the reporters' frenzy," Megan said. "It will be impossible to go anywhere without a tail."

"We'll help," Saber said. "Don't worry. Your few days away will be private unless one of you suffers from foot-in-mouth disease."

The press pursued them home, but Gerard closed the gate at the end of the long driveway, halting their chase. Megan wanted to cheer as the gate shut behind the last of their vehicles. The childish part of her wanted to poke out her tongue, but she restrained the urge.

"The first time we've ever shut the gate," Gerard said.

They'd arrived back at the house together. Henry had ridden with them while Gerard and London drove in their own vehicle. Leo and Isabella Mitchell, Gerard and Henry's friends, arrived soon afterward. Leo was lending

Jacey his SUV for the next week and returning her rental car for her.

They were a friendly bunch, and apart from the reporter situation, Megan had enjoyed herself. She'd arrived with low expectations and had a ball. None of them gave her the celebrity treatment or treated her as if she were an exotic creature. It was...nice, she decided.

"So, where are you and Jacey going?" Isabella asked. The blonde wore an edge of determined intensity, yet Megan didn't think she meant to use the information for her own gain.

"I don't know. He won't tell me." Megan couldn't believe how calmly she was taking this organization. Normally, she liked to keep tabs on her schedule and give herself an exit strategy. With Jacey, she didn't worry about him doing anything underhand, but she wasn't one-hundred percent sure why she trusted him. It was a gut thing, yet she'd never trusted her instincts to this extent. Weird, but she could envision a time when she might even confess she wrote torrid paranormal romances under a penname in her spare time.

That had never happened before.

In the large kitchen and dining area, London dispensed glasses of wine and bottles of beer. She pulled two containers of homemade dip from the fridge plus a plate of vegetable sticks and crudités. From the cupboard, she grabbed a large packet of crisps and dropped them into a bowl.

Megan's phone vibrated, and she pulled it out of her pocket to glance at the screen. She'd left it turned off during the matches. When she'd powered it back up again, it was full of messages and texts from colleagues and other media contacts wanting to know the gossip. Those she ignored. This latest call, however, she didn't want to consign to her trash.

"I need to return this call," she said to London. "I'll be back soon." She headed to Jacey's suite and locked the door after her, not wanting any interruptions. Not that she thought any of them would try to eavesdrop, but she didn't want to take chances. Commonsense told her to take this slow even if her gut told her this was right. Stupid gut instinct.

"Hi, Janet. What's up?"

"You remember we were talking about ghostwriting? I have a job for you. It's not ghostwriting He wants someone to write his biography for him. Doesn't have the time or the patience to do it himself."

Excitement burst in Megan. "Okay. Who is it?"

"Strangest thing," Janet said. "The guy was born in New Zealand but didn't hit it big in pop and country until he moved to the States. Dillion Grieves. Have you heard of him?"

Who hadn't? Extraordinary songwriter with a type-A personality. "Didn't he have a recent stay at rehab?"

"A wake-up call, he told me. He wants to write his life story to prove anyone with a dream can achieve the same success with hard work. His purpose is to let young people know it is a mistake to rely on drugs and alcohol to get through dark periods. He said if he can save one person from making the same mistakes he did, it would be worth it. Guy sounded sincere, and even better, he's in New Zealand for several concerts next week. I told him about you and he wants to meet."

"Sounds good. I'm not sure what is happening at work yet and won't know until after my holiday, but it won't hurt to speak with this guy."

"Good. I'll arrange it and get back to you. Evening meetings work best for you?"

"Yes, either that or breakfast meetings."

"Done. Oh, you need to keep quiet about this. He wants no one to learn about this project before he is ready."

"No problem."

"How is it down in the country? Did you get to plan B yet?"

Megan grinned. "I did."

"Oh? Tell me more."

"No. Not right now. I don't want to spoil things."

"Should I check the online gossip for your part of the world?"

Megan shuddered. "No."

"Ah!" Janet sounded delighted. "That means I should. I can't wait to see what you've been up to."

Megan groaned. "Let me know about the schedule, and I'll make it work." She hung up to Janet's delighted laughter.

The phone rang again. Rowena, her job replacement. No. She refused to speak to her. Megan sent the call to voice mail and left her phone on the bedside table. While she couldn't in good conscience switch it off right now because her sister might call, she could ignore her calls and check on them periodically.

Megan made her way back to the kitchen and found that the party had moved to the lounge. A fire burned in one of those modern fires that looked as if logs were burning but it was all an illusion. The heat was welcome though, since it had rained as they left the sports grounds.

"Everything okay?" Jacey asked, his face brightening when he saw her. He stood and came to meet her, his good manners giving her the warm tinglies.

"A work thing," she said, keeping her answer vague. "It's a meeting I need to attend after my holiday."

Jacey guided her to the couch where he had been sitting. "Is wine okay for you or would you prefer something different?"

"I can control myself around wine, you know."

"That's good to know," Henry said from across the other side of the room. "I'd hate to fend you off again, or worse, face Jacey because he caught us kissing."

Gerard and London cackled.

"Embarrass me again, why don't you?" Megan chided. "I was having an atrocious day."

That set the tone for the rest of the evening. There was joking and teasing and she learned about local gossip and about the various neighbors and family members.

"Do you have family in Auckland?" Isabella asked.

"My sister and her husband live just out of Auckland. I don't see them as much as I'd like because of my work commitments. Tessa is having her second child any day now. That's why I can't turn off my phone."

"You don't want to spend your holiday with her?" Jacey

148

offered her a guarded smile, as if he dreaded the answer.

"No, Tessa doesn't expect me to hover. She says she has several sisters-in-law for that. I'll visit once the baby arrives and send a welcome baby present."

"Hey, Isabella," Leo said. "It's time for us to head home. Do you need help to confuse the press tomorrow morning?"

"Yes please," Jacey said. "Thanks for lending me your vehicle. Once I get back, I'll purchase one of my own. I can't keep borrowing vehicles."

"There's no hurry to get it back." Leo stood and held out his hand for his wife. "We'll get to wave at the reporters as we drive past in Megan's flashy rental. They might take our photo."

"I hope not," Isabella said. "Last thing I need is more women chasing after my gorgeous mate."

With thanks and goodbyes, the couple left. London cleared empty bowls and glasses, a big yawn stretching her jaw.

"I can tidy up for you," Megan offered.

"I'm not intending to do more than rinse the dishes and put them in the dishwasher, but I wouldn't mind an extra set of hands to cart them out to the kitchen."

Megan helped London, then poked her head back into the lounge where the men were discussing a Super Rugby match. "I'm off to check my phone, so I'll say good night."

"I'll be there soon," Jacey said, his blue eyes lighting with heat.

"Good night, Megan," Henry called.

"See you in the morning," Gerard said.

A blush crawled across her face at the accompanying wink from Jacey, the act hurling her back into the past and her relationship with Charlie. They'd been so happy together. High school sweethearts. They'd planned their future. Decided to wait for the kids. Then he'd gone to Afghanistan and hadn't come home. Her smile stuck to stiff lips as she turned away.

Things would've been so different if Charlie had lived.

She entered Jacey's suite and walked through to the en suite. They'd stopped to pick up her clothes and to check out from the cottage, and her cosmetics and toiletries mingled with Jacey's. Something she'd never had with Charlie. A simple thing that shouldn't make her weepy, yet it did.

The outer door opened and Jacey's reflection appeared in the mirror with her. His initial smile faded.

"What's wrong?"

She turned to face him and gave him a watery smile. "Do you think about your wife sometimes?"

"Of course I do. We had a good marriage. Henry reminds me of Moira. His smile. He smiles, although you wouldn't know it. The way he tilts his head."

"I became engaged to my high school sweetheart when I turned twenty. He's been on my mind today, since I met you."

"What happened?"

She swallowed. "He died in Afghanistan. He was a soldier."

"Aw, Megan." Jacey took her into his embrace and wrapped her in a sympathetic hug. "It's natural to think about your fiancé, especially since you've landed feetfirst in a relationship with me. You went through a lot together with your fiancé. What was his name?"

"Charlie."

"And?"

"You." She hesitated then went with honesty. "I've never clicked with anyone as well as I did with Charlie, not until you. It's put me off my stride, made me doubt myself."

"Instead of worrying about the future, why don't we enjoy our time together?" Jacey brushed a fingertip over her cheek, then traced it around her lips. A tingle sprang to life and frisked her body in a visceral reaction, pulling her nipples tight. Her gaze lifted to connect with his, and the heat in his strange eyes weakened her knees.

He wanted her. *Her.*

Not her public persona. Her fame and well-known face didn't seem to impress him at all.

"We've known each other for mere days. We have five more days to spend together, to see if we fit and want to aim for more. There is plenty of time to talk and get to know each other."

The urge to bite her lip became too strong for her, and she caught her bottom lip between her teeth, worrying it as she attempted to calm her racing fears. She wasn't sure if she should trust her instincts about him. That was what it came down to—a difficulty to trust this man who was essentially a stranger. Charlie's death, the other men in her life who had disappointed her, leaving her alone.

She'd wanted children at one time. Now it was too late because she didn't want to be that elderly mother waiting at the school gate.

"Megan." Her name was whisper-soft, yet held a tinge of order. "One day at a time. Please, give us a chance."

She nodded. "I'm normally more decisive."

"We all have our moments." Jacey kissed the tip of her nose, the corners of his eyes crinkling. "All I ask is you keep an open mind. Don't decide that this is wrong between us because it's happening so fast. If you want to walk away, do it now. Please."

A lump filled her throat, making her swallow and swallow again. A chill prickled her arms and legs. Fear. It stood up and howled through her mind—a mournful howl that sounded like a wolf.

She shook her head and the despondent cry ceased. Her gaze rose to meet his again. "I can't leave. If I walked away now, I'd always wonder about what might have been. I'd be a coward, and the last thing I want to do is be a scaredy-cat full of regrets."

"Which means?"

"I might have doubts and concerns, but I want to relax and spend the next few days with you. That is my last word on the matter."

"Do you have a bikini?"

Her brows rose at the change of subject. "I have a two-piece."

"Close enough. We might have time to do a day trip to Tekapo. Have lunch overlooking the lake. Swim in the hot pools there. What do you say?"

"I've only visited the main centers in the South Island through my job—Christchurch and Dunedin. I'd love to see more."

"Good." He pulled away and held out his hand. "Want to share the shower with me?"

The quick punch of a memory—an old one where she and Charlie shared a tiny shower together. To save water, he'd said, but they'd groped and caressed and kissed, getting themselves off before they hit the bedroom. So long ago. A memory with so much hope for the future.

"Yes," she said decisively. "You start while I clean off my makeup. I'll be quick."

"We won't hurry," he replied. "This shower might take time, and once we're done, we'll have a do-over in bed."

A shiver worked through Megan. "Sounds like a plan." She reached for her cleanser and began her evening ritual. Behind her, Jacey started the water running, and his clothes rustled as he disrobed.

Some of her worry dispersed.

One day at a time.

She wiped the cleansing milk off her face with practiced strokes of a tissue, then pulled off her clothes. She opened the glass door to the shower and stepped under the warm water.

Jacey grinned with approval. "You were quick."

"You didn't believe me?"

"Moira was never on time. Never. It was one of her charming quirks."

Instead of the jab of mental pain, at the mention of Moira, she smiled. "Charlie was always early. Used to drive me crazy. Do you have any flaws you care to admit to?"

Jacey took his time answering, squeezing shower gel

onto a washcloth. "I get cranky sometimes and need space before I regain my balance. I go for a run, and that clears away the blues. You?"

"I eat too much chocolate, and I have a fondness for the white stuff, which isn't chocolate at all. When I have downtime, I pick up a book. These days my e-reader since I can carry my entire library with me. I have a terrible book habit. My office at home is full of bookshelves, all overflowing. I need more, but there is no space to put them."

"Hmmm," Jacey said. "I like books. Mostly nonfiction."

"I read romance, but I'll deny that if you repeat the information. I'll deny everything."

A rumble of humor shook Jacey's frame. He pushed her wet hair away from her face and tipped her head up so he could kiss her.

And that was the last of the talking they did. They confined their communication to groans of appreciation, silken touches and erotic whispers. His mouth was hot and wet against her neck, and the lazy stroke of his tongue against the sensitive cords had her pulse racing. The gentle suction of his mouth and his skillful hands that skimmed with purpose, with skill that had desire stirring, tugging at her pleasure points.

Her nipples hardened beneath his questing fingers, and a hungry little noise rushed past her pursed lips as his hand cupped her mons. One blunt finger traced her seam and sparks of pleasure followed in the wake of that digit. Her breath caught, and she widened her stance.

"I enjoy the way you respond to my touch. It's not

practiced, as if you have a routine." He nipped at the base of her neck. "Your reactions are real." Jacey maneuvered her against his chest and whispered against her ear. "I want my cock inside you. Want to feel your snug warmth again."

His soft words, erotic and blunt, had her inner walls clenching. "Yes," she agreed.

"One problem. I forgot to bring a condom with me."

A gurgle of laughter escaped her. "I didn't bring one either, and I'm Condom Girl. London's words, not mine."

Jacey chuckled. "I love the girl. She's perfect for Gerard."

"So what do we do?"

"We work around the limitation." His finger circled her clit and a buzz of sensation had her catching her breath. He ran his finger lower and dipped it inside her. He licked the shell of her ear when her head fell back.

"Jacey," she whispered. It normally took her longer to warm up, but this...this was something else. Breathtaking and decadent. And those sinful lips of his. His finger invaded and retreated, invaded and retreated while his other hand rolled a nipple. His lips and teeth continued to kiss and nibble. He cajoled and captivated and whispered to her in a husky voice.

"I want to feed my cock to you, see your lips wrapped around my girth. Want to do so much with you, to you, but most of all I want to shove into you until neither of us know where we begin or end."

His voice was velvet rough, his finger continually moving, filling her, driving her pleasure higher. He nuzzled her neck, bit down lightly, and she exploded—a short, sharp climax that left her gasping and shuddering.

Jacey turned her to face him, his eyes that deep blue with an underlying amber tinge. She was learning that when his eyes looked like this, he wanted her. Her lips curved. As if she needed the additional info. His cock was a hard spike against her backside.

Jacey turned her around to face him. "I want a comfortable bed for my next move."

Megan stared at him, her gaze flickering down to his erection.

"But first we'll finish our shower." He added shower gel to his washcloth and rubbed across her breasts, then her belly. The water poured down, cleansing away the fragrant suds. Megan lifted her face to the water while Jacey washed his own body.

"Done?"

"Yes."

He flipped off the water and reached outside the cubicle to grab the two navy-blue towels waiting for their use.

Five minutes later, clean and much dryer, Megan sat on the edge of the bed, combing her hair. She glanced up to meet Jacey's intense gaze.

"I want you."

"We have condoms now," she murmured. "Why don't you let me explore you first?" She crawled toward the middle of the bed where Jacey reclined and ran her fingers across one hip, over the ridges of his abs. Hard muscles. Her gaze skimmed his erection. All the man was hard, and she'd never seen a man this in shape since Charlie. Most of the men she'd dated after Charlie were businessmen or retired sportsmen who ate as if they were still in training.

Unable to resist, she reached out and traced a light finger along the length of his engorged cock. His hips jerked upward and into her touch.

"Want a little more pressure?"

"Yes." His eyes glittered with challenge.

She nodded and straddled his hips, flushing when his focus went straight to the juncture of her thighs.

"I enjoy your blushes."

"How do you know I'm blushing?"

"Your gasp. It's a tell with you."

"Never," she said. "I didn't gasp."

"Yep." He regarded her, a teasing light in his gaze, and she melted inside.

When he looked at her that way she felt as if she was the most important thing in his life. Crazy, really, since three days ago, they'd been strangers.

"Now that I'm at your disposal, what did you intend to do with me?"

Without warning velvet tension swirled through the bedroom. Their gazes connected and heat flared in her. "Why, I thought I'd explore. I told you that."

"Still waiting."

We'll see about that. She leaned over and rasped her tongue over one flat nipple. His swift intake of air brought satisfaction and a desire for a repeat of the sound. She rubbed her fingers over his other nipple. Back and forth. Back and forth.

Jacey stroked her hip, and she lifted her head to wag her finger at him. "Hands at your sides, palms flat on the mattress," she said in a stern voice.

The corners of his mouth turned up a fraction as he obeyed her orders.

"Much better."

His mouth quirked higher at her comment, and she bit down her own laughter.

During their lovemaking to date, she hadn't taken the time to explore his big body and the faint dusting of hair on his spectacular chest. Her fingers trailed over the hard planes, testing the muscles.

"How do you keep in such great shape?"

"I run," he said.

She flicked his nipple and grinned when he jumped. His cock jerked against her backside. "And your job? What exactly do you do?"

"Computer security plus whatever Henry and Gerard need help with. Sometimes I'm a security guard or I fit alarm systems."

Still didn't explain his peak physical condition. "Have you always done security work?"

"I was in the military for a while."

Ding. Ding. "A while ago?"

"Until Moira became sick."

She bit her lip, sorry that she'd raised the subject. "I'm sorry."

"Don't be. Moira and Charlie will always be a part of us. It's natural." He lifted one hand and tweaked her nose. "Seems you have a thing for military guys. Ms. Saxon, do you have an army bias?"

She pinched his nipple, and a dark sound rasped from his throat, his eyes going that amber blue she liked. Very much.

Megan lifted her body and moved toward his feet. Her fingers gripped his cock, and she caught the flare of desire in his eyes. Then, a thought roared through her like a bullet from a gun. Hello. Naked. Body on display with the lights on. Horror layered on top of the want in her, almost buried her for an instant. What was she thinking? Putting herself on display.

"Is that all you will do?" he asked in a gritty voice that pierced her tumultuous thoughts.

She gasped in air. His scent, her scent, wove around her senses, calming her panic.

"Megan?"

"What would you like?" Somehow she got the words out, hoarse and sharp-edged, past the gravel in her throat.

"Give me your mouth, woman. Your smooth, warm hands. And get that look off your pretty face. I know when a woman is worried about her body."

Her head fell forward, her chin to her chest. Her heart thundered, a rush in her ears that almost overcame good sense.

"Megan?" This time her name was a sharp slap through the pregnant silence.

Every sense seemed to magnify. Her hearing. The smells in the room. And when she glanced up, her sight seemed sharper, despite the film of tears in her eyes. She found Jacey staring at her, arrested and focused. There was a growling buzz inside her head that just wouldn't shut up.

She pressed her fingers to her temple. "I'm sorry. You're seeing the worst of me this weekend. I've cried. I've tried seduction. I've embarrassed myself. And now it appears I learned nothing because I'm rinsing and repeating!"

Jacey moved so quickly, she didn't even see the intent telegraphed in his expression. She found herself wrapped in his embrace, his heart beating against her breast. He ran a hand down her back, soothing and stroking, as if she were a wild beast. In her mind, she chortled like a mad woman at the thought. But the thing was—his touch soothed her, pushed away the fears that prowled her mind.

He kissed her cheek, her chin, her nose, and the fears settled like content dogs, fading away the more he touched her.

"You don't need to apologize. Everything in your world tilted upside down after you learned about the job. You're off-balance and it's understandable."

"I'm an idiot."

"Maybe," he said and there was a smile in the word. "But tonight you're my idiot."

The pleasuring stroke of his fingers continued. His mouth trailed down her neck, then she shivered beneath the roughly sensual bite and play of his teeth. Sweet agony flared to life at his touch, the stirrings of arousal driving off the last of her anxiety.

He rolled her and cupped a breast, splayed his fingers over her stomach. Craving kicked in her belly, a primitive throb jolting through her veins. His mouth sought hers again with tiny kisses, tantalizing but brief. A muscular thigh slid between hers as he took her lips with more passion, exploring her mouth with his tongue. She moaned and stretched against him in an insistent rock for more.

"That's my girl," he whispered in approval.

He pushed her onto her back and parted her legs again before leaning over to grab a condom from the open box they'd left on the bedside cabinet. Competent hands stroked his shaft and rolled on the protection.

Megan tensed, knowing she'd need more foreplay. The older she got... She opened her mouth and found him smiling.

"Hey, I'm not a brute. Trust me, okay?"

His gentle, understanding tone flustered her. He patted her outer thigh and reached over to slide open the drawer. Curious, she glimpsed a small bottle, but he moved in that lightning-quick way of his. He parted her legs and lifted her to his mouth. Before she could marshal her thoughts, he had his mouth on her. A sensuous lick stole her breath, caused a tightening sensation deep in her womb. She swallowed, her mouth dry, her heart thudding and a body that flared with sensual flames.

His breath misted against her clit while the stubble on his jaw rasped against her delicate inner thighs. Raw need pulled at her as his tongue circled her entrance and a finger teased her nub. Unbidden, her hands dug into his hair and her hips jerked upward. The man played her body, pushed the right switches to drive her arousal.

A finger pushed into her channel, and despite her fears, she took him easily. A second finger joined the first, the easy plunge and retreat vibrating internal pleasure points. How had she coped before Jacey? The man took such care with her, treated her like a treasure and that, in return, seduced her.

When he withdrew his fingers, she moaned in complaint.

"Shush."

He straightened and picked up the discarded item he'd taken from the drawer. A slim black container. With a wink in her direction, he took off the lid and squirted something into the palm of his hand before placing the container aside again.

"Close your eyes."

Her eyelids felt like weights anyway, so it was easy to obey. Immediately, her other senses stepped up to broadcast information. The bedclothes rustled beneath Jacey as he shifted his weight while his addictive scent—that wild outdoors scent full of trees and freshness—pulled at something deep inside her.

A blast of chill against her clit jolted her, the icy shot morphing to heat that swirled through her, swamping body and mind with pleasure. The delicate stroke of his finger against her nub followed by a light pinch sent an exquisite shot to her sweet spot. She gasped, and the sequence repeated. Chill. Heat. Pleasure. Chill. Heat. Sultry promise. The third time caused flutters in her channel. Sweet, sweet, tension.

"Jacey," she cried.

"Perfect," he whispered. "I wish you could see yourself as I do. Your beautiful breasts." He pinched one at the same time as he ran a finger around her clit. "Your swollen clit poking from its hood, the deep pink folds of your pussy." He chuckled at the wet sound of arousal. "The matching roses in your cheeks. I think you're ready for my cock now."

His dirty talking threw her, yet she loved the way he told her what he wanted to do, what he saw.

"Jacey." His name was a plea.

"Do you want me to fuck you now, Megan?"

"Yes."

"Tell me what you want, sweet pea."

Oh heck. He wrecked her when he called her sweet pea in that tone. The combination of desire and command. "I want you to put your cock in me."

"Sweet pea, it will be my pleasure."

No, she suspected it would be her pleasure first, because the man wasn't a selfish lover. Her breath came in ragged bursts, her eyes still shut.

His touch disappeared for an instant, and her pulse thrummed in urgency.

"I want your eyes open this time."

She obeyed before she voiced the question. "Why?"

"I want to see your eyes as I fill you." His cock surged into her, thick and hard, his gaze intent on her.

Another series of chills and heat sparkled across her flesh, and she realized he'd coated his condom-covered erection with whatever was in the container.

"Beautiful," he whispered in a hoarse voice.

Clawing tension pushed and pulled at her. A rumble of a growl filled her mind, and his quick grin told her she'd issued the sound. He pulled back and surged into her again, the width of him stretching her inner walls. Goose bumps prickled over her but not from the cold. Blistering waves of heat delighted her while the clawing pressure in her lower belly frustrated her. Each of her muscles jumped at his touch, and the unbearable friction just kept growing and growing.

He paused, fully seated, to kiss her with just the right amount of pressure. A harsh sound of animal enjoyment rippled from her, and he laughed against her lips.

He fucked her harder, faster, surging into her wet core. The tendons of his neck stood in stark relief, as if he was holding part of himself back.

"Yes," she insisted, moving her hips to meet his thrusts.

He gave a feral smile and snapped his hips, plunging his cock into her heat, driving her pleasure up, making her fly. With a cry of surrender, she convulsed around his cock. He growled, raw and guttural, as the tension snapped into a thing of raunchy beauty.

His lips crushed hers in a statement of intent, of ownership even, and her channel clenched around his cock in a smaller series of ripples. He gave a rough and raw growl, and his cock pulsed. He slid in to the root and stayed, a hard jolt deep inside her sending another series of spasms through her. He nipped at her throat, the sensual bite whipping her with pleasure.

Jacey's heart thundered against hers, and he sought her lips even as she smiled at the jolts of his cock deep in her body.

Pleasure still writhed through her, and even though Jacey's bulk bore down on her, the last thing she wanted was to move. This seemed right. Her life leveled out when she was in Jacey's arms.

Her eyelids lowered and her mind drifted.

"You okay?" Jacey whispered.

"Mmm."

He whispered. "Me too."

For an instant, she thought a trace of worry wove through his words, then she consigned that thought to the trash because he kissed her, a soft lover's kiss.

She sighed and yawned, tiredness fogging her mind.

A long time later, Jacey separated their bodies. She thought she heard him curse, but no, that couldn't be right because he kissed her shoulder again. Megan liked his kisses. She liked Jacey Anderson very much.

Chapter Ten

Shock rippled through Jacey as he pulled free of Megan. *That* hadn't happened before. Of course, rumors circulated, but it had never happened with Moira. He pulled off the condom—the ripped condom—and stared at Megan. Her cheeks still flushed from their lovemaking, her hair mussed and she'd never looked more beautiful to him. She stirred, but it was obvious if she wasn't fully asleep, she would be soon.

With caution, he prodded the end of his cock, the wolf's barb still protruding enough for notice. He winced at the tenderness and groaned. What the fuck was he going to tell Megan?

The truth. The rapid thought came through in the soft cadence of Moira's Irish accent. How did he tell Megan that his wolf had claimed her? The loutish brute.

Jacey sighed, not unhappy with the situation, but confused and out of sorts with the suddenness of his wolf's pounce and his inability to halt the action. He'd already known he and Megan were compatible on a cellular level. Her scent and his over-the-top attraction, his responses to her had informed him of that, but he'd hoped for time. Not...not this ambush by his wolf.

He padded to the en suite to discard the condom and wash up. He should wake Megan and confess—at least about the broken condom. No, she'd only worry. Morning was soon enough. They could visit Gavin, the feline doctor and local vet, to get a morning-after pill, if that was what Megan wanted. He sighed. Something else to explain—why they would visit a vet for a medical crisis. Perhaps he should call Gavin, explain the situation and the hovering press, ask if he could make a house call. Yeah, that would work.

God, he needed a drink. About time he got in some supplies. He'd have to brave the communal kitchen, and he wasn't sure he was in a state to chitchat. Another glance at Megan told him she would sleep for a while and wouldn't notice his absence. Stealthily, he pulled on his jeans and left his suite.

The kitchen and dining area lay in darkness, but one sniff told him he wasn't alone.

"Henry, why aren't you sleeping?" He slid onto the barstool beside his son. Hell, he had to talk to someone. It looked as if Henry was *it*.

"Why aren't you in your bed? You have a sexy woman to keep you entertained."

"She's asleep." Jacey heard the sharp note in his tone and cursed under his breath. "Sorry." Jacey climbed off his stool and headed for the booze. "Want one?"

"Can't have the old man drinking alone."

Jacey snorted. "Not so much of the old." He sloshed a healthy measure of whisky into two glasses and carried them back to where Henry sat.

They sipped in silence, which should've been restful. Jacey's mind churned like a concrete mixer. He sensed Henry's gaze on him, adult somber, and so unlike the kid he remembered.

"Want to talk about it?"

"Yes. No." Jacey's shoulders slumped. "I don't know."

Henry groaned. "Bloody hell. You have a sex problem. You're right. I'm the kid. I don't need to learn about my father's sex life."

Jacey spluttered out a laugh. "You weren't that keen when I was trying to explain sex to you either. You got over that."

Henry sipped his whisky.

"I can't talk to anyone else. It's a wolf thing."

Henry's glass rose again, but he held it in front of his face instead of drinking. Yeah, he had the kid's attention now.

No easy way to say this. No matter how he did it, he'd be off-balance, a touch mortified.

"You've heard rumors of some wolves having cock barbs?"

Henry twisted on his stool to goggle at him.

"Hell," he muttered. "You're making me feel like prey."

"Go on," Henry said.

"I always thought they were just that—rumors and gossip to titillate. Turns out the tales are true. My barb ripped off the end of the condom and dug deep into Megan. My wolf just took over, and I had no control. No disrespect to your mother, but the sex was incredible."

"What did Megan say? Is she upset?"

"I don't know," Jacey confessed. "The intensity of the sex seemed to knock her out, and she was half asleep even before the barb released."

"So she could be pregnant?"

"If the stories are true."

"Hopefully she's in the wrong part of her cycle."

Jacey's hand trembled as he lifted the glass to his mouth. "My wolf doesn't think so."

"What are you going to do?"

"I don't know, but I can't lie to her about the condom. Once she's conscious, she's likely to realize something isn't right. I could have woken her, but there was no point worrying her. There is the morning-after pill. I'm hoping Gavin will do a home visit."

"Gavin has studied more about wolves since I arrived," Henry said. "He might have come across something in his research."

"Yeah."

"You could always ask her to marry you."

Jacey shook his head. "It's too soon. We've known each other for mere days. She has her job in Auckland and travels for her work. I'm committed to staying in Middlemarch."

"You could always go with her to Auckland."

"My wolf hates cities. We do much better if we can shift on a regular basis and run. Being moon-called is a pain in the arse during these modern times."

"True," Henry said. "It's a luxury avoiding the forced shift at full moon. I mean, mostly I still shift then because I can, but the odd time I can't it doesn't matter because my wolf is satisfied with the regular shifts."

Jacey puffed out a breath. "I hear you. It's part of the reason I didn't hesitate to organize a few days' break with Megan, even with the full moon close. My wolf is like a lazy puppy at present instead of a hungry stray."

Henry barked out a laugh. "That's the sex."

Jacey hid his grin behind his glass. "That too."

"You could confess about the condom, offer her the alternatives, which as I see it are: one, the morning-after pill; two, wait and see what happens because she might not get pregnant; three, termination at a later date. As for the other—your wolf might have claimed her, but you haven't done a blood exchange yet."

"The tie between us exists already. I sensed it before this happened. Now it feels stronger. The blood exchange is a mere formality."

"You don't do things the easy way."

"Nothing about this is easy," Jacey agreed. "Megan is the first woman to grab my attention since Moira. I like her a lot." He drained the last of the whisky, savoring the burn down his throat. "I might go back to bed. Thanks for listening."

"Dad?"

Jacey stilled beside his stool, emotion tightening his chest. "Yeah?"

"No matter what happens, I have your back."

Jacey reached over and embraced his stepson, a wave of love filling him. "Thanks. See you in the morning. We might be late for breakfast."

Henry squeezed him in return and pulled back. "Nah, I think you want to avoid your turn cooking. You're meant to cover for London, remember?"

MEGAN WOKE SLOWLY, WARM and rested after the best sleep she'd had for days. Without haste, she rolled over, searching for Jacey.

He was already awake, gaze subdued. "Morning, beautiful."

Pleasure filled her on hearing his husky greeting. "Have you been watching me?"

"Yes."

"Is something wrong?" Something in his expression started her stomach roiling. She swallowed and licked her lips to moisten them.

Regret chased across his features, a flicker of apprehension.

"Is there a story in the paper about us? In the gossip section?" That might explain his behavior.

"No, I don't think so."

"Oh. Well, that's a relief." She would have expected a story after the fuss the press had made when they left the sports ground.

"The condom broke last night."

She gaped at him. "The condom?"

171

"Yeah, it broke."

"Oh. Oh!" She bolted upright, her mind still groggy as she strove to make sense of the repercussions. She counted. Crap, she was in the right part of her cycle.

"Given the circumstances, the local doctor would be willing to make a home visit. He could give you the morning-after pill."

"No." Her answer was instant and came from part of her brain that wasn't completely online yet. She'd always wanted children, and while a broken condom wasn't an ideal method of conception, she couldn't destroy a possibility.

His brows rose. "No?"

"I-I...why didn't you tell me last night?"

"You dropped off to sleep, and I figured I'd give you a few hours without worry."

"Oh. What do you want me to do?" She couldn't read him, couldn't discern the way his thoughts headed. The morning-after pill, a termination—no. Neither was an option for her—not if she was pregnant. Her mind shuffled through her options. Only one choice she found acceptable.

He winced, let her see the sliver of pain in him before he answered. "I will support whatever decision you make." Sincerity blazed in him.

This man would stand behind her decision. She believed him in a heartbeat.

"If I'm pregnant—"

"If you're pregnant, we will be together and I will offer support and my love. Megan, I'm halfway in love with you now. You make me happy."

He sounded so confident, so certain of his mind. Most men would sweat this calamity.

She wanted to hug him for his support. "I'll have to return to Auckland, for a short time anyway."

"I can't live in a city, Megan. I've committed to helping Henry and Gerard, but even if I hadn't, city life isn't for me."

"No, that's not what I meant. Heck, I don't know what I meant—just that I have to go back, make decisions, whether the broken condom has consequences or not."

If she didn't return to her job, and this weekend had made her consider the alternatives, she'd turn to writing. She could ghostwrite and work on her own books. She could coach a rugby team, something she'd always wanted to try. A baby...

She crawled off the bed and went to him, took his hands in hers. "I always thought I'd left it too late for a child. Charlie and I...well, we wanted children. If I'm pregnant, then I'll wait and see. Termination—no, that's not for me. Financially, I could cope with a child."

"I would help."

If she didn't return to Auckland. "I don't want to see a doctor. Not yet." She squeezed his hands. "I might have a shower."

Jacey nodded. "Do you still want to spend time with me?"

Megan considered days of loneliness, stress too, as she made plans for her future. At the very least, Jacey could listen and offer suggestions. "I haven't changed my mind.

I'm not sure how soon pregnancy tests work, but if it's soon, we can do that together."

"Thank you."

She paused at the en suite door. "Why?"

"You haven't screeched at me or blamed me for the broken condom. I suspect most women would."

Jacey waited until the shower switched on before pulling on jeans and a T-shirt. He'd have time to cook breakfast after all.

He found Henry in the kitchen again, making a start on French toast. "Did you sleep?"

"A little. How did it go with Megan?"

"If she's pregnant, she wants the baby. She seemed calm. Didn't cry or shriek." Maybe too calm.

"You should know in a few days, right? Her scent will shift before a pregnancy test is viable. Will you let me know?"

"You'll be the first one to know. We'll hit you up for babysitting duties. Think of this hypothetical child as payback."

Henry cracked five eggs and beat them with a whisk. "I wouldn't mind a brother or sister. How come you and Mum didn't have more kids?"

"It didn't happen for us, then Moira became sick. You want me to grill the bacon?"

"Yeah, and put on the coffee. I could do with a cup."

"I need another whisky. Guess I'll make do with coffee."

"Morning, Pop." London breezed into the kitchen with

Gerard a few steps behind her. "Smells good. Have you worked out your great escape yet? I did a load of washing and hung it outside. Gerard helped and said he could hear the reporters at the gate."

Huh! The reporters were the least of his problems this morning. Somehow, he had to woo Megan and persuade her to stay in Middlemarch. His happiness and that of his wolf depended on his persuasion prowess.

Maxwell's Resort, Cromwell, South Island

Megan was pregnant. Jacey smelled the change in her scent and everything in his world shifted yet again. Although part of him had known—suspected—confirmation struck him with panic. An adult shouldn't have this type of mishap, yet a part of him thrilled with excitement.

A child.

A permanent tie to Megan.

His wolf stirred, prowling his mind and pushing at his control. The knowledge excited his wolf, and his feelings for Megan—hell, he was so close to loving her, he might as well call it by the correct name. He loved Megan and wanted her and the baby in his life.

It was meshing their futures that was the problem. Megan still intended to go back to work. She said she wasn't sure what they'd offer her, but she owed them the courtesy of listening to their vision of her future. And she had a business appointment, arranged by her agent. He still wasn't clear why she needed an agent and she'd been vague on the subject.

After one day of rain, the weather had cleared to a sunny morning. He glanced at Megan who stretched out on a deckchair, a book in hand and his worries eased.

"Want a drink? A tea or coffee?"

She placed the book facedown on her lap.

Jacey came to an abrupt halt. *Wolves*. She was reading about wolves and their behavior?

"Is there any fruit juice left?"

"No, but I can ring reception. Or we can go for a walk. Good book?" He thought he'd slid his question into the conversation naturally.

"This? I like to read non-fiction. Wolves are fascinating creatures, and I feel an affinity for them."

She bore a wolf scent, even stronger now. Curious.

"Want to walk to the café down the road instead of ordering in? It's a nice day, and no one has bothered us while we've wandered around town."

"Yes, please. Their blueberry-and-white-chocolate muffins are scrumptious. I wouldn't say no to one for morning tea."

"After that huge breakfast?"

Megan laughed. "I'm blaming you for all the exercise, both in and out of bed."

"You complaining?"

She closed her book and stood, her lips curling into a sassy smile as she leaned closer to kiss him. "Never. I've never felt better."

"You look beautiful. More rested than when you

arrived."

"I've caught up on my sleep. That always helps. Now about that muffin. I'm ravenous all of a sudden."

He remembered Moira saying how much food she'd eaten while she'd carried Henry. Unable to resist, he slapped Megan on the backside. "Let's move then, before they sell out of their muffins."

She shot him a reproachful look and headed indoors to collect a hat. "The chocolate ones aren't as tasty."

"Don't forget your glasses." Jacey slapped a cap advertising Perth on his head and reached for her hand. "You can tell me all about wolves during our walk because I find that anything that fascinates you, interests me too."

"I like reading about big cats. Leopards and lions. Mythological creatures like dragons intrigue me and I've always gravitated to myths and legends. Ghosts and things that go bump in the night."

"Yet you ended up with a career in sports. You could have gone ghost hunting or become a zoo keeper."

"You're teasing me. How did you end up in security?"

Jacey entwined their fingers once the path leading to the front gate of the resort widened. They passed pots of lavender, bare of flowers given the season. Henry had told him they usually had snow by now, but the one light cover they'd received in Middlemarch hadn't lasted for long. Only the tops of the hills bore the whiteness of winter snow.

Once they exited the gate, they turned to the right and walked along a hedge-lined lane.

"My father was in the army and I followed in his

footsteps."

"Didn't your parents worry about you?"

"I'm sure they did. Just as I worried about Henry. It's a parent's job to worry about their children."

"If we have a child..." She trailed off, her expression one of anxiety. "I'm worried that if I am pregnant, you'll leave me. I..." She waved a hand, as if shoving her spoken words out of the way. "Forget I said that."

Jacey stopped walking and turned to face her. He cupped her face in his hands. "I'd marry you in a heartbeat. The only reason I haven't mentioned it already is because we haven't known each other for long. I thought we had plenty of time to get to know each other and work through the other obstacles."

"My job?"

"And my preference for Middlemarch."

"I feel different here. I don't know whether it is my imagination or something else."

Jacey squeezed her hand, wishing he could level with her, but his mind told him it was too soon. He needed to approach their relationship carefully, or he'd scare her away. "We could stop by the chemist while we're out walking, although I checked the internet. A few days after your first missed period is best for the test."

"I'm going crazy with the not knowing, but it's too soon then."

"I'll just have to take your mind off the topic. What do you say to an afternoon snooze before we head off to dinner at that historic pub later this evening?"

"Plan," Megan said and resuming walking, reaching for

his hand of her own volition. He rather liked her fingers wrapped around his.

Once she learned the truth—the fact she was pregnant—he hoped she'd still want him around. He didn't know what he'd do if she rejected him.

Megan stared at the pregnancy test, purchased from the local chemist shop. The girl who had sold the kit to them had said it was too early for an accurate result, but a positive result showed on the stick. She was going to have a baby. She stumbled out of the luxurious bathroom holding the stick in her right hand.

"I'm pregnant."

Jacey stood and went to her. He enfolded her hand in his and led her to a navy-blue two-seater. He sat beside her, his arm loosely wrapped around her shoulders. "Are you okay with that?"

"I—we're both older. What if we embarrass our kid at the school gate because we're old?"

Jacey barked out a laugh. "We can work around that problem. Not that I think it is one. No, are you okay with being pregnant?"

Concern lined his face, glinted in his pretty eyes and her heart squeezed. "I think I'm fine with it, which is strange given the circumstances," She tested her mind and a smile slid into place along with happiness. "I'm excited."

"Good."

One word, but it shimmered with emotion. They grinned at each other.

"Do you feel up to a nap?"

"No, I don't want a nap." A gurgle escaped at his disappointment. "I want to have some hot, steamy sex."

"Vixen." He followed this up with a kiss that smoked her insides. Passionate and caring, hands wandering, shaping, tormenting her. He cupped a breast, and desire kicked in her belly. This man—what his touch did to her. She shuddered under his attentions, her travel to arousal swift and sure. Maybe it was the pregnancy. Maybe it was Jacey. Maybe it was a combination of the two. All she knew was that this twist, this wrinkle in her smooth-running life, should bring a burst of fear and anger, yet happiness came in its place.

And she realized something. Contentment filled her—more than she'd experienced for a long time.

CHAPTER ELEVEN

LATER THAT NIGHT. DINNER, CROMWELL PUB

"THIS IS A GORGEOUS place," Megan said as she glanced around the tables, set with white tablecloths, sparkling glasses and silverware. "And the view is incredible. I'm glad we came early, so I can still see a little of the surroundings." She turned to take in the panorama of green fields stretching out before them, the lights popping on to combat the growing darkness. The pub crouched on the edge of a hill, the historic building erected during the time of the gold rush. A gas fire burned in the center of the room, flames flickering between logs that looked real.

A beanpole-thin waiter with dark hair and a beginner's mustache showed them to a table for two, situated to take in the view. He gave them menus and filled water glasses. "The special tonight is roast lamb with rosemary potatoes, Brussel sprouts with chestnuts. This comes with a homemade mint sauce. Would you like something to drink?"

"We'll have a bottle of sparkling water," Jacey said.

The waiter nodded and hustled away to deal with other diners.

"I'm not going to drink alcohol, but you don't have to abstain."

"The bubbles are to celebrate. I might have the odd drink in the future, but not tonight."

Megan reached across the table for his hand and squeezed it. They weren't married, but this man drew her with a magnetic force. She wanted to keep him. The revelation gave her pause.

The sensible part of her snapped ramrod straight and started to lecture. *So quick. Too quick. How can we trust him?* The romantic part of her stood toe to toe and did a loud raspberry.

She scanned her menu. "If the food is as good as it smells, we're in for a treat. I'm craving meat. The lamb sounds good, but I think I'll go for the steak."

"I'll take the lamb and you can try some of mine," Jacey said, reminding her of Charlie in that moment. They might not resemble each other, but at heart, they bore the same gentlemanly manners and pure heart.

So there, her romantic part said and did another raspberry.

"We need to make plans," Jacey said, his manner tentative.

"We do," Megan said. "I've been thinking about the

future. This is what I'm thinking. I have to go back to speak with my employers and work out my notice."

Jacey gave her a slow smile. "You've decided to resign?"

"Yes, travel during a pregnancy will be too difficult. Following the Sevens tournament for example would have me flying all over the world. Hong Kong. Dubai. San Diego. South Africa. Japan. And that's only a few of the destinations. It's tiring even at full fitness. I have another offer I can't tell you about, but I could do the majority of the work from home with minimal travel. If it's okay with you, I think I could live in Middlemarch."

"Yes," he burst out, his grin broad and lighting up his blue, blue eyes. "That's wonderful. We can live with Henry and Gerard or we can buy land nearby and build. Whatever you want."

"The setup you have is good. I thought it would be weird, but your suite is private and I love the communal feel of the rest of the property. London is a sweetheart, and we'd have built-in babysitters."

"If we're in Middlemarch, we'd have those anyway," Jacey pointed out. "What about Henry? Is it weird living near my son?"

She thought about it. "I like Henry and Gerard. The only thing that is lacking is an office. I'll need an office."

"Ah, but we have a spare room next to London's office. We're using it for storage at present, but we might rearrange things."

A sudden burst of emotion forced tears to her eyes. A big, fat tear rolled down her cheek and plopped onto the tablecloth.

"Megan, are you crying?"

A second tear rolled free. "I'm s-so happy." She fumbled in her handbag for a tissue.

The waiter chose that moment to arrive with a bottle of sparkling water. He frowned, his eyebrows lifting as he poured the water into their glasses. "Is everything all right?"

"We're fine," Jacey said in a husky voice. "We'll have the steak done rare and one roast lamb please."

"Starters?" the waiter asked.

"The meat platter," Megan said and dabbed at her eyes.

"Very good," the waiter said after noting their selections on his order pad.

"I hope he hurries," Megan said. "I'm so hungry I can hear growling in my head."

Jacey's expression shifted again. *He's worried*. Another wave of something close to love slipped through her in an embracing wave.

He rose. "I'll be back in a minute."

As she watched, he headed deeper into the restaurant and around the corner toward the restrooms. Her phone rang then, and she plucked it from her handbag, scanning the number and smiling.

"Hey, sister mine. Have you popped that baby yet?"

"Not yet. He's hanging in there and I wish he'd get on with it. I resemble the rear end of a hippopotamus."

"Lie," Megan said. "Stewart loves you. I think you look gorgeous. Definitely a lie." Although she was bursting to tell Tessa the news, she remained silent, not wanting a lecture about being irresponsible and worse. Besides, it was

184

early days, and anything could happen. She'd watched her sister with her first pregnancy. She'd lost the baby weeks into the pregnancy, so she'd wait. Megan ignored the spike of pain in her chest at the thought. Despite the unexpected conception, she *wanted* this baby.

"When are you coming home?"

"I'll be back in three days. Tuesday." She glanced through the window and glimpsed the moon. The pale globe glinted a gorgeous creamy color, mesmerizing her with its beauty. Almost a full moon, Jacey had informed her the previous night as they'd sat on their deck, wrapped in a cozy woolen blanket. She didn't know why but it drew her. Always had. "I've decided to resign from my job."

"What? But I thought this was the job of your dreams?"

"It is...was. They shifted me sideways when they gave Rowena the job on the new sports show. I'm not sure what they envision for me. I'll talk to them when I return, but I've moved on."

"What will you do?"

"Not sure yet," Megan said, keeping her tone light. "I'll explore the options and let you know. I won't have time to drop by on Tuesday, but Wednesday night for dinner. How about if I bring something for dinner?"

"Don't forget I'm vegetarian."

"How could I? How does Thai sound? That way I can have my meat, and they'll have something vegetarian for you. Stewart eats both so that will work."

"Perfect."

Megan smiled. They were so different, her and Tessa. She'd developed itchy feet and loved the outdoors, red

185

meat, while Tessa was the polar opposite, loathing meat and preferring indoor pursuits. It was true Megan wrote, but she spun tales of fantastical creatures who were rough and tough and embraced the outdoors and their animal natures. Her mother, who was more like her sister, had despaired of her tomboy ways. Her father used to encourage her.

"I'll see you on Wednesday then. You tell that baby to hang out until I arrive." Her sister's groan was still echoing down the line when she disconnected the call.

"Work?" Jacey asked as he joined her.

"My younger sister. Her second baby is due any day, and she feels as if she's ready to pop."

"Did you tell her—"

"No, I want to wait a bit longer until I'm sure everything is all right."

"I don't think I'll be able to stop myself telling Henry, but he'll keep it a secret."

She understood Jacey's eagerness. It had killed her not to trumpet the news to her sister that she, too, would be a mother—all going well.

The waiter arrived with the meat platter and set it in the middle of the table. He gave them a plate each, topped up their water and left.

Jacey speared a piece of sausage and a testy growl escaped her. He laughed as he offered it to her.

The meaty treat filled her mouth with spices as she bit down. She swallowed, unable to meet his gaze. She'd growled at him.

"What next? One of these beef slices?"

"I can feed myself."

He didn't reply but arranged the beef on his fork and held it in front of her mouth. The meaty juices burst across her taste buds, but this time she held back her rude growl.

After the fifth bite of meat, she felt more balanced, some of her hunger pangs appeased. "You'd better eat some before I polish off the entire platter meant for two."

"You go right ahead. I like seeing a woman enjoy her food."

Megan stopped with her fork halfway to her mouth. "I like you so much. You always say the perfect thing to set me at ease."

"I like you too," Jacey whispered, his gaze heated. It skimmed down to her neckline and the thrust of her breasts, and she could have sworn she felt the gentle tickle of his fingers.

"I have a secret," she announced, her mouth in gear before her brain approved the concept. But no. She sensed he'd never rat her out. "You remember that book I was reading on wolves."

He stilled, his gaze unblinking. "Yes."

"I wasn't just reading it for interest. It was research."

"Oh?"

He stared at her with his magnetic blue eyes, and she had no idea what he was thinking.

No idea.

"I had a lot of downtime—at airports, in hotels, on planes—and I started writing books. On a whim, I sent one to an agent. I write paranormal romance under a penname. The book on wolves is for a new series I'm developing about werewolves."

At this, he blinked once. His thoughts remained a mystery, but at least he hadn't guffawed or treated her like an idiot. She'd heard her male colleagues' discourse on girlfriends and wives who read that sappy dribble.

"Werewolves, huh?" He finally broke the silence. "I take it you're published."

"Yes."

"Can I read one of your books?"

"So you can poke fun at me?"

"Never," he said and his tone made her believe him. "London reads romance. She might have one of your books."

"I can bring you my author copies when I come back to Middlemarch."

"I'd like that. Are you going to tell me your secret name?"

"Carrie English."

The waiter interrupted, arriving to remove the empty platter.

Once he'd left, Jacey reached for her hand. "I think that is wonderful, and your secret is safe with me. Can you tell me about your werewolf books?"

"Still in the research stage. I'll let you read the first draft when I'm done. If you're truly interested and aren't going to poke fun at me."

"Never," he said. "Have you read up on werewolf mythology?"

"I was hoping to track down books at Auckland library. I like to do my initial research at the library rather than on the internet. It was easier to tote along a book on the plane, although I have apps to save information so I can read without being online."

"There are a couple of books on my bookshelves that might help. Actually, they might still be in storage. Moira and I both liked to read. I'll hunt them out for you."

Her heart gave another one of those stupid clenches and her eyes prickled with the beginnings of embarrassing girly tears. Jacey didn't fit the mold her mind had made for the men in her life. After Charlie, no one had seemed good enough, although she'd tried. Jacey—he was making his own mold. One she liked very much.

Chapter Twelve

Thursday, the following week

Jacey sat at the kitchen counter, his iPad in front of him. He scanned an online bookstore and hit search, his curiosity driving his quest. How he'd lasted until now—he had no idea.

"Looking for something, Pop?" London darted up beside him like a jack-in-the-box, and he—a big, bad wolf—hadn't heard a thing.

He scowled at her. "Don't do that creeping thing."

Her eyes widened. "I prowled." She beamed. "Gerard says I walk around with the stealth of a herd of elephants. No elephants that time. What are you so engrossed in?"

"Have you heard of Carrie English?"

"The author?"

"Yeah." Jacey risked a glance at London, saw she wouldn't poke fun at him and relaxed.

"I have some of her books. She writes romances with

dragons mostly, although she has written series featuring feline shapeshifters. It's kinda cool reading them now that I know shifters are real. How did you hear about Carrie English?"

"Megan mentioned her. I was curious about how writers portrayed shapeshifters and werewolves in genre fiction." Heck, his explanation impressed him.

London grinned. "Gerard likes me to read the sexy bits aloud for him. He says that Megan smells different. Is there a reason for that? I asked Henry, but he had a phone call and we got interrupted."

Jacey reached over and tweaked her nose. "Haven't you ever heard that curiosity killed the cat?"

"The cat learns nothing if she doesn't ask. Want a coffee?"

"Yes, please. I'm waiting for a phone call about some parts before I go to Dunedin to collect them. Want to come for a drive?"

"Sure, it will give me time to pump for info about you and Megan." Her impish grin pulled an answering one from him. "She is coming back?"

"Yes," Jacey said, satisfaction filling him at the idea. He missed the woman, having her in his bed. In the short time they'd been together, he'd come to enjoy talking to her about anything and everything. It differed from the discussions he had with Henry, Gerard and London.

"Pop." London shook his shoulder. "Just making sure you were still here. You looked as if you drifted somewhere else."

"Can I borrow your Carrie English books?"

"You want to read them?"

"Yes please. Don't tell Henry."

"Of course I'm gonna blab to Henry. That's half the fun."

"You tattle to Henry and I won't tell you a single secret."

London flapped her hand in patent unconcern. "Pooh. You're no fun." She plunked a coffee in front of him. "I wouldn't mind doing a grocery run if we're going to Dunedin. Will there be time?"

"We'll make time," Jacey said.

Half an hour later, they were in Gerard's SUV on their way to Dunedin.

"Carrie English has a new book out. I haven't had time to read it yet."

"I'll buy it for you. Can we get a copy while we're in Dunedin?"

London wrinkled her nose. "Most of the shops don't stock romances. I order mine online. In the past, I've bought print, but I think I'll ask for an e-reader for my birthday. Storage is becoming an issue. I'd better write a list. Can you think of what we need?"

Jacey glanced in the rear-vision mirror. "I thought most of the reporters left with Megan."

London turned in her seat. "They're following us?"

"Yes."

She shrugged. "Let them. We're picking up parts and going grocery shopping. Nothing interesting about either of those things."

Once they reached Dunedin, Jacey used the GPS to find the warehouse specializing in security products.

"Do you want to come inside?"

"I'll wait here," London said. "Can I play with your iPad? I was wondering whether to get one instead of a dedicated e-reader."

Jacey handed it over. "You should be able to get the internet. Download a book to read if you want. Don't go nosing through my emails. You might get embarrassed."

London pulled a face. "Spoilsport. Can I read an online newspaper?"

"There's a news app there somewhere. I've been avoiding the local news since I got sick of seeing my picture." He shuddered, and it wasn't pretense. Not just the tabloids, but even the traditional papers had run a story on him and Megan. He glanced out at the street and spotted the car that had followed them all the way from Middlemarch.

It took Jacey longer than he expected.

"Sorry," he said after he'd loaded the parts in the rear of the vehicle and climbed behind the wheel. "Henry rang for me to add extra items to the order."

"Pop," London said. "You'd better take a look at this."

After all the teasing, her serious demeanor had his wolf pricking its ears. "What is it?"

"A new story about Megan."

He took the iPad, his gaze fastening on the screen and the photo of a laughing Megan with a younger man, their heads close together as if in an intimate conversation. The wolf growled loud enough for London to stare at him in apprehension.

London squeezed back against her seat. "I'm sure it's

193

nothing."

"She said she had a business meeting last night."

"There you are then." London bit her bottom lip, her blue eyes full of concern.

"She didn't mention the meeting this morning." She'd told him she was going to the doctor first thing then she was doing an interview.

"Ring her. Ask her about the picture," London said. "There is no need to grump and growl at me for the rest of the day. Gerard and Henry would tell you the same thing. If there is something going on, confront her."

London made good sense.

"You know how the press slants stories and pictures to sell papers," she added.

Also a good point. His wolf ceased his loud rumbles, confining himself to an upset whine. Megan had the power to cut out his heart. He told himself there was a good explanation for this photo. It looked nothing like a business dinner, yet his hand trembled as he hit speed dial.

It rang several times before it went to voice mail. He hung up without leaving a message.

"No reply," he said in a terse voice.

"Pop, I thought it was the right thing to show you the photo, but I don't think Megan would do that to you. You said she is coming back to Middlemarch."

London was right, but pain pulsed inside him like a nagging tooth. And his whining, complaining wolf had his head thumping.

"Let's get the shopping done." Jacey started the SUV and backed from the parking space.

"I downloaded Carrie English's latest book and started reading. I think you'll be able to follow the story okay even though it's a series."

Jacey gave a clipped nod, his hands gripping the steering wheel so hard it was a wonder it didn't crack.

"The white car is following us."

Jacey glanced in the mirror. "Now we know why."

In the supermarket carpark, the reporters made their move. Two skinny, bearded men ran up to them, one with a camera and the other carrying a microphone. "Have you any comment about Megan Saxon ditching you for a younger man? Did she tell you she was seeing Dillion Grieves?"

London's fingers twined around his and tugged to get him moving. Blindly, he followed, grateful for her intervention when his wolf rode him so hard.

"Mr. Anderson, don't you have anything to say about Megan Saxon?" the reporter persisted.

"Don't say a thing," London whispered. "No ammunition."

The reporters ran after them, nipping at their heels and reminding him of pesky bugs. With bugs, he'd fumigate. Couldn't do that here. Not the thing to make a scene. *Wolf, back.*

The whining and growling had him pressing at his temples.

London gasped and squeezed his hand tighter, making him realize he'd grown claws. Fuck.

He increased the length of his strides, and London scurried to keep up.

"Just as well, I'm fitter these days," she said, gasping for breath as they burst through the front entrance of the supermarket.

"I'll get a trolley," he said, his tone close to a bark.

London, to her credit, didn't flinch. She pulled out her list and directed him to the fruit and vegetable aisle.

The reporters didn't back off. The photographer's camera clicked and whirred. Great. Both still pictures and video. The man with the microphone kept barking questions at him. Nosy, obtrusive questions.

Megan carried his baby. She wouldn't betray him in this manner.

"Does Megan know about Dillion's drug problem?" the reporter demanded, dogging their heels all the way to the potato and onion section.

"That bag of potatoes," London said with a jerk of her chin at the trolley. "A bag of those red onions."

"Does Megan know you're playing house with this woman?"

Jacey turned at that, anger blazing. His wolf would show in his eyes but he didn't care. The reporter blinked, and the connection broke when London slipped into the gap between them.

"He is my father-in-law, you disgusting weasel." Her crisp English accent cut the air with the precision of a blade. The whispering huddles in the vegetable aisle silenced, eyes and ears in their direction. "We have nothing to say to you, and if you don't leave us alone, we will complain to the supermarket management."

A man in a suit rounded the end of the aisle and headed

for them. "Is there a problem?"

"Yes," London said. "We're trying to do our grocery shopping and these two...people...are bothering us."

"I will escort them off the premises," the man said. "This way, sir." He gestured at the reporter.

The reporter drew himself up. "We have every right—"

"Grant," the cameraman said. "We have pictures. We can work with those."

The reporter gave a clipped nod before turning to Jacey and London. "You can run but you can't hide."

The mockery prodded at Jacey's wolf. He held himself together. Just.

"Pop, let's finish our shopping. Do you fancy leek and potato soup this week?"

With the reporter and cameraman gone, Jacey's wolf settled, but he was aware of the other shoppers pointing at them, whispering behind their hands.

London linked her arm through his as they neared the meat aisle. The blast of cooler air from the chillers helped him bat back his wolf who subsided, finally, with a grumpy snarl.

"We have plenty of meat, but I like to check out the specials. How do you feel about roast chicken for a change?"

"I think I need alcohol or chocolate," Jacey grumbled, and London relaxed, her brittle smile turning into something more natural as she placed two frozen chickens into the trolley.

"How about we do some baking and make bread once we get home? You can pretend the dough is a reporter."

Jacey snorted but followed London down the baking aisle. He'd taught Henry how to bake bread because all the kneading and punching had helped to calm his wolf and he'd thought it might help his son in times of need. And the fact they'd both enjoyed homemade bread didn't hurt.

"Focaccia bread," he suggested. "It will go good with the soup."

Back in the SUV, with the groceries loaded, Jacey tried Megan again. His call went straight to voicemail.

"Send a text," London suggested. "Ask her why she's hobnobbing with famous singers. Tell her I want to know if he's sexy in person."

"Casual and non-confrontational."

"Yes," London agreed.

An excellent plan and not his first instinct. He'd intended to snarl at her and demand answers. This was better. Much better. He typed in the message and sent it. "Thanks," he said gruffly. "I couldn't have a better daughter-in-law."

A blush of pleasure filled London's face. "I don't exactly have competition for the job. No doubt I will in the future." Her cheeks paled again as she thought of her sister and her untimely death.

At least, that was what Jacey presumed. "Gerard is lucky to have you."

"Thanks," she whispered.

Jacey put the SUV in gear and took the road for Middlemarch. At least the reporter had vanished, and they wouldn't need to deal with them again today.

· ♥ · ♥ · ♥ · ♥ · ♥ ·

LATER THAT DAY, EXECUTIVE Suite, Barret Hotel, Downtown Auckland

"The job is yours, Ms. Saxon," Dillion Grieves said. "I've asked my agent to contact yours with the contract."

"Thank you. You'd better call me Megan since we will be working together. One more thing I'd better tell you before the final contracts are signed. We discussed doing the interviews via skype and some in person. That's still fine, but I'm pregnant, and I won't be up to travel later on in my pregnancy."

"Crap," Dillion said.

"Problem?" Megan asked coolly.

"The paparazzi grabbed photos of our dinner meeting. My agent told me when we spoke, but I haven't seen them. He said they look intimate. Is that going to cause problems?"

"Ah, I wondered why I had so many messages. I was running late after visiting my sister and didn't have time to check them. I'm an auntie again." A thrill went through her, both for her sister and for her coming baby. The doctor said she was in great health and had given her a referral to a doctor in Dunedin.

"Will your man be upset?"

Megan paused with her fruit juice halfway to her mouth. "If I were him, I'd be irked."

"I'd be pissed," Dillion said. "But then, that's me. I have a temper."

"I'll ring him as soon as we're finished," she said.

"I've asked for a confidentiality clause in the contract, but if you trust him to keep quiet, you can tell him the truth about our meeting."

"I would have told him anyway," Megan said, realizing she trusted Jacey. The man was honorable and had more integrity than most people of her acquaintance.

Dillon narrowed his eyes.

"I will do the work at home. He will see my notes and research. Jacey isn't stupid. He can add one and one."

Dillion nodded, after a long pause in which he assessed her intently. "Fair enough, but he opens his mouth and tells anyone, I'll sue. No one else must learn of it until just before release date. I want to surprise the public and give them a week to clamor for the book and speculate. That is my plan."

"I understand." Megan held out her hand, and they shook. "If you can swing it, there is a place on the outskirts of Middlemarch that often hosts celebrities. They have security and look after their guests. You could stay there. Middlemarch, the town where I'm going to live, is a small country town. The locals have been good to me and they haven't talked to the reporters."

Dillion tapped a long finger against his chin, his gaze distant as if in thought. "Shania Twain has a property down that way. Wanaka somewhere, I think."

"Think about it. You could fly into Queenstown. It's smaller and you're less likely to attract attention, especially if you keep a low presence."

Dillon nodded. "I'll consider it."

Ten minutes later, hotel security held back the reporters

as Megan climbed into a taxi. She'd intended to walk the short distance to her apartment. The press made that impossible. Instead, she studied the moon through the window of the cab and admired the way it glowed on the dark waters of the inner harbor.

CHAPTER THIRTEEN

JACEY SAT IN THE lounge with Henry and Gerard, idly watching the Super Rugby final between the Hurricanes and the Lions. A New Zealand team versus a South African team. The final and he couldn't focus on the plays and darting runs of the backline.

His phone rang, and he glanced at the screen. *Megan*. The underlying tension simmering in his gut turned up in heat.

The two boys glanced at him, and London appeared from the direction of the kitchen.

"Aren't you going to answer it, Pop?" she asked.

Henry pushed pause on the game. The phone rang again.

Jacey answered the call. "Hey, sweet pea." The taut tone echoed the tightness in his muscles.

"Jacey, I've missed you. I have great news. Three pieces actually. My agent just confirmed it. I'm writing Dillion

Grieves biography. The press took photos of us together, although I guess from your text you've already seen them. The project is hush-hush, so you can't tell anyone else. I had to sign a confidentiality clause and can get sued if the word gets out."

Jacey's muscles unclenched. His breath whooshed out of him. "T-that's great news. I won't say a word to anyone." He glanced at Henry and Gerard and waited for them to give him quick nods of agreement. London wouldn't have heard Megan's words with her human ears. "And the other two things?"

She laughed. "The doctor confirmed I'm pregnant and in good health, and I'm coming home tomorrow. I've still got to finish packing, but I've arranged shipping for the important stuff. Can you pick me up at the airport tomorrow? My flight gets in at eleven."

"I'll be there," Jacey said. "I'm going to be a dad."

"Me too. A mother, I mean. How cool is that?"

"Very," Jacey whispered, not even caring that the kids could hear everything. "I miss you."

"Ditto," Megan said. "Eleven tomorrow. I'm saving a big hug for you."

"I'll need more than a hug," Jacey said.

"That could be arranged."

Jacey hung up with a smile as he heard the slight gagging sounds coming from Henry.

"Pop," London said. "Did I hear right? You and Megan are having a baby? What went wrong? I thought you used condoms?"

Henry sprang to his feet, crossed to the chocolate-brown

two-seater where Jacey sat, and hauled Jacey to his feet for a hug. "I suspected, but you said nothing, so I kept quiet."

Gerard nudged Henry aside to give Jacey a hug too. "Huh! I had my suspicions too. I didn't say anything because neither of you did."

Henry returned to his seat, the boy appearing happier than normal. Geoffrey trotted over to Henry and nudged his hand in a demand for a pat.

"Hey!" London had her hands planted on her hips. "How did you suspect?"

"Megan smelled different last time we saw her," Gerard explained.

London wrinkled her nose, her chin lifting as she gave her mate attitude. "You could've whispered in my ear."

Gerard winked at her. "I believe we were busy doing other things."

Jacey watched the delightful surge of color creep to London's cheeks, obscuring her freckles. "You're the first human I've told and amongst the first officially given the news."

"Well," London said, appearing mollified. "I guess that is okay. Is Megan staying in Auckland? Are you a couple or are you friends?"

"Megan is coming to live in Middlemarch." Jacey felt his chest expand—puff out, in truth—and wanted to punch his fist into the air. Instead, he dropped onto the two-seater and leaned back against the cushion, arms spread wide. His sigh held happiness.

"Does Megan know about shifters? About werewolves?"

"No." His satisfaction dispersed like a balloon-pop at London's question. So much had happened in a short time. He hadn't wanted to tell Megan the truth about his origins until he'd felt more certain of her. Now, a baby tied them together for the foreseeable future. "I'll tell her, of course, but I wanted to wait and speak to Gavin about any problems that might occur."

London went to Gerard and slipped her arm around his waist. "No matter when you tell her, Pop, it will be a shock. Tell her she can talk to me if she wants. Will the baby be a werewolf?"

"No." Faint regret filled him at the truth. "Wolves differ from felines. When a wolf mates with a human, the genes are diluted and the offspring can't shift."

London leaned into Gerard. "When we have kids, they'll be able to shift to feline, right?"

"Yes." Gerard kissed the top of her head.

"When we first met Megan, I thought she smelled of wolf," Henry said. "It's stronger now, but that's your scent imprinted over hers."

London frowned. "I don't understand. How is that possible? Why would you pick up a wolf scent from her?"

Henry resettled on his chair and picked up a bottle of beer. "She must have an ancestor who bore werewolf blood. It's more common than you'd think."

"So when is Megan coming back?" London asked.

"Tomorrow at eleven. Can you boys do without me for the day?"

"Why don't you take a couple of days?" Henry asked. "We have that big job next week, but nothing Gerard and

I can't handle this week."

"No, I've already taken days off. Megan won't mind. She'll have her own work to do. She'll need office space. Can she take the spare room next to London's office? Can we rehouse the parts somewhere else?"

"There is room in the warehouse. It makes better sense to have all the parts together," Henry said.

"Why does Megan need an office?" London asked.

Jacey tapped the side of his nose. "She might tell you." He grinned. "The woman is full of secrets."

"I will be filling in at Storm in a Teacup for Emily during the next week. Morning sickness is hitting her hard, and Saber wanted her to dial back at the café for a while. Tell Megan she's welcome to use my office until you can set up something for her."

"Thanks," Jacey said.

"Is my good nature and kind offer worth the trade of a secret?" Her impish smile tugged an answering one from him.

"Ask Megan. I'm not confessing any secrets."

"Don't think I won't," London said.

"Are we going to watch this game or what?" Henry pushed the start button without waiting for a reply.

Jacey watched the players toss the ball from one side of the field to the other and the Lions team tackle them hard, but instead of following the game, his mind drifted. Megan was coming home and it couldn't happen soon enough.

THE NEXT DAY, DUNEDIN airport

Megan smoothed her hand over her long brown hair—a cheap wig, purchased last year for a fancy dress party—and after pulling on a cream merino beanie, exited the plane. She sent a text to Jacey. *I've arrived. In disguise. Brown wig. Cream beanie. Red handbag. Jeans and cream jumper.*

Her phone beeped seconds after she sent her text.

Also in disguise thx to London. Black hair. Jeans. Purple/black jacket. Waiting at arrivals gate.

"Great minds," she murmured, earning a curious gaze from a pair of teenage girls. They took one look at her and sniggered, heads pressed together. Clearly, they considered talking to one's self a sign of madness.

Ignoring them and the other passengers, she hefted her computer bag, repositioned the long strap of her red handbag over her shoulder and increased her speed. She'd been gone longer than she'd expected, found the break from Jacey painful. Understandably, Tessa was concerned about the rapid manner in which Megan was changing her future. She'd argued that just because Megan was pregnant, she didn't have to move to a small town that was nothing more than a dot on the map.

Megan had regretted spilling the news about the baby to Tessa, given the lectures she'd received in return. She hadn't meant to, but excitement had her blurting out the news during a visit to see Tessa's new baby. Anyone would think she was the younger sister. Megan pushed aside the hurt caused by the friction. Tessa thought Jacey had hit on her because of her fame, and she'd made her disapproval of the recent gossip regarding Megan and Dillion Grieves clear.

Frustration ate at her as she recalled their heated conversation. Unable to defend herself or explain, she stood there, stinging under the lash of Tessa's censure. She strode into the arrivals' hall and scanned the expectant faces.

"Hey, pretty lady."

She whirled on hearing Jacey's voice, blinked a fraction at his appearance, then threw herself at him. His muscular arms welcomed her, and she leaned into his strength.

He pulled back when someone jostled them from behind and took her hand. "Let's collect your luggage and get out of here. Let me carry your laptop bag." He held out his hand.

She hesitated because she'd had another casual interview with Dillion, and she'd hate anyone to get hold of her notes.

"Confidential stuff?"

His voice held no judgment, and she nodded.

"No problem. I understand."

Relief beat a tattoo through her veins. Tessa would have pitched a blue fit. She had lashed out when Megan refused to discuss her meeting with Dillion. It was true that Jacey had learned the truth about Dillion, but he wasn't pushing for more and she appreciated his trust. "Thank you." She pressed a kiss to his cheek. "I missed you. My bed felt lonely."

"I'm so glad you're here."

Jacey organized her luggage and fifteen minutes later, they were on their way to Middlemarch.

"You know," she said as they drove up the long winding drive to the house. "I have the urge for a nap."

"Are you tired?"

"Not especially." She scanned the house, turned to Jacey and everything inside her welcomed and embraced the sensation of home. The entire time she'd been away from Middlemarch, a low-level anxiety had kept her on edge, her thoughts on Jacey and how it felt with the miles between them. "I missed you so much."

"Do you need to go back to Auckland?"

"Not in the near future. I think Jeremy was relieved when I handed in my notice because they didn't know what to do with me now that they've given Rowena my job. I thought the poor man might expire when I knocked on his office door and asked to speak with him."

"Will you miss your job?"

"I'll miss the people I worked with and the rugby, but I'll have different challenges now. I'm excited about the biography and I can work on my own books, start my new series. Then there is the baby. I think I'll have plenty to do."

There was no one in the communal rooms when they entered the house.

"Where is everyone?" Megan found she'd missed them too—the charming Gerard and his bubbly wife, London, and Henry. If their baby turned out anything like Henry or Gerard, she couldn't help but be a proud mother.

"London is filling in for Emily Mitchell at the café. Emily is suffering from morning sickness. The boys are out fitting security lights at a new business in Hyde."

"So we have the house to ourselves?"

"For the moment."

She yawned—a fake one—and burst out laughing at Jacey's expression. "I'm not really tired, but I need you. I've been imagining making love with you for the entire flight from Auckland."

Jacey muttered a low curse. "Work can wait. Let's go." He dragged her through the communal rooms and into his suite.

Their suite.

Megan gave a delighted laugh and followed without hesitation. Jacey set her bag down and turned to her. He prowled toward her, gaze intent and, laughing again, she backed up until the bed halted her retreat. Before she could decide what to do next, he jumped her. They fell back onto the bed in a tangle of limbs. Their lips met, and neither of them left the bedroom for a long, long time.

THREE WEEKS LATER

"Hey, Jacey," Henry said. "Gerard and I are going for a run with Leo and Isabella Mitchell. Do you want to come? We're leaving in half an hour."

Jacey considered and gave a quick nod. "Just let me tell Megan I'm going out for a bit."

"You told her yet?"

Jacey sighed, "No. I've started to half a dozen times, then I chicken out or the subject drifts."

"You haven't claimed her properly?"

"No, I wanted to give her time before I mark her."

One similarity between cats and wolves. Both species bit their partners on the marking site—the pad of flesh at the base of the neck where it met the shoulder. Once the marking occurred a stronger bond developed between the mates, and only death parted them. Moira and he had both worn each other's mark, and he'd mourned when his had vanished after her death.

Now, however, it was more than fear of losing a mate that ate at him. What if Megan couldn't accept his wolf, accept that their baby would carry wolf blood, even if he or she never shifted? They would pass that blood onto their children.

"Jacey—Dad—she is a good woman. I like her. Gerard and London like Megan too. We enjoy having her around, and I like seeing the way you are with her. You're happy and not as serious. Put your trust in her and tell the truth."

"You're not telling me anything I don't know, but telling her opens me up to rejection. I don't think I can handle that."

"Mark her then. Give yourself an advantage."

Jacey stared at his son. "I've considered it," he said in a hoarse voice, shame making his shoulders slump. "It's not the act of an honorable wolf. I can't trap Megan that way."

"Just checking," Henry said in a mild voice.

"A test?"

"You passed. I knew you would."

"I'll tell Megan I'm going for a run." He laughed when Henry gaped at him. "Megan assumes I'm running with two legs. See you in five."

Jacey went in search of Megan and found her in

211

London's office. London was working in the café again and doing some of her virtual assistant work during her down time.

"How is the writing coming?"

"I've been reading through diaries today and taking notes. I have an online interview session with Dillion at the end of this week." She stretched her arms above her head and groaned. "I must be coming down with something. I feel achy. Nothing wrong with my appetite though." She pulled a face. "I'm craving a steak."

"I'll take a couple out of the freezer."

"Already done. London has a chicken ready to go into the oven." She glanced at her watch. "Almost time to put it on to cook. I told her I'd put it on for her if she wasn't home in time. Chicken sounds good too." Her stomach rumbled in punctuation of the thought. "I hear Emily Mitchell is eating a lot of vegetables and staying healthy. I'm eating meat that is barely cooked. Are you sure the doctor said that was okay? It doesn't seem healthy, but I can't stop myself."

"Gavin said that the body has a way of demanding what it needs when a woman is pregnant. He said as long as you remain active and don't feel ill, not to worry."

A horn honked.

"I'm going for a run with the boys. That okay?"

"Of course!"

"Gotta go," Jacey said when the horn honked again.

"Have fun."

"We'll be away about an hour. Don't overdo it." He kissed her, smoothed his hand over the slight bulge of her tummy and left at a jog.

Megan brushed her fingers over tingling lips. She hadn't realized the stress she'd carried on her shoulders with her job. Living in Middlemarch didn't bore her. If anything, the social whirl exhausted her, but it was fun too. She stretched again and winced at the deep ache in her bones. It was worse than she'd let on to Jacey, but she hadn't wanted him to chastise her for carting boxes of research around. Now she was paying for her foolishness.

She scooped up the stack of diaries and her notes and locked them away in a safe Jacey had procured for her. Security contacts came in handy.

A hot shower might help with the aches and pangs. She turned off the computer and left the office in darkness. The security lights flicked on to light her way to the house, darkness setting in early now that they'd hit mid-winter.

Instinctively, her gaze sought the moon. A weird obsession. Harmless but weird. She huffed out her amusement. She *was* turning odd in her old age. Her hand went to her stomach to cup the slight mound. "Kid, not only are you going to have older parents but a peculiar mother too. Two strikes against you already."

She hurried inside and shut the door against the cool night air. How Jacey and the boys could run in this cold, she'd never understand. In the communal lounge, she turned on the gas fire. Chicken next. She turned on the oven to heat, made a cup of mint tea while she waited and picked up Jacey's tablet to check her email. *Ooh, her new cover. Nice!*

London arrived home about half an hour later, and Megan climbed off her barstool to make her a cup of tea too.

"You don't have to wait on me," London said as she took the stool beside Megan. But she cupped the mug of tea and sighed in appreciation.

"What do you think of this?" Megan asked and slid the tablet over for London to see her cover. A man with a broad chest, tattoos and the faint impression of dragon scales screamed bad-boy attitude on this most recent cover. It fit well with the rest of the series, and she liked it very much.

"What are you doing...how did you get to see a Carrie English cover? Are you in her fan group?"

"No." Megan giggled. A nervous chortle from she who never uttered a girly giggle.

"Then how..." London's eyes went wide. "Jacey asked me about Carrie English books. He wanted to read one."

He'd read the love scenes out to her in his sexy voice and seduced her with her own words. A whoosh of heat eased the ache in her bones and muscles.

London's gaze narrowed, and Megan could see the younger woman's brain ticking over the information. "You're Carrie English." Distinct accusation rang out and echoed in the kitchen.

"Guilty."

"Why don't you have a newsletter? You don't even have a fan group."

Megan suppressed her grin. "I didn't have time to do

online promo or any promo with my work schedule."

"You're hiring me," London ordered. "I will organize everything for you. And don't think I'm giving you family rates either. You can't keep a huge secret like that from family."

"Tessa, my sister, doesn't know. She doesn't approve of trashy romances."

"Even if her sister wrote them?"

"That would be worse," Megan said, no longer suffering pangs of hurt at her sister's attitude.

"Can I read this one early? Before the rest of your fans?"

"You really enjoy them?"

"You will autograph my collection. I'm moving into e-books because of storage and it made little sense to get all my books sent over from England. I had to choose my favorites, and my friends freighted them here for me."

"I'd like to keep my pen name secret," Megan said.

"Why did you tell me?"

"You said it earlier. You're family. I'll tell Gerard and Henry, but no one else. Jacey already knows."

"I won't tell anyone," London promised. "But I'm serious about the promo thing. Can I work for you?"

Megan held out her hand. "We'll shake on it." With the formalities sealed, Megan relaxed as London chatted with her about promo. A yawn slipped free before she could cover her mouth. "Sorry. I'm starving but I'm not sure I can stay awake for dinner."

London checked the clock on the microwave. "Why don't I cook you a steak then you can head off to bed? Jacey and the others won't mind if you go to bed early."

"I can cook a steak."

"You're exhausted. Stay there. It won't take me a minute to organize a meal for you."

"You've cooked all day. You shouldn't have to run after me."

London turned to her. "If I were pregnant and tired, would you cook a meal for me?"

"Of course I would."

"There is your answer then. The minute I'm pregnant I'll expect breakfast in bed. At the very least," London announced.

The younger woman moved around the kitchen with ease, pulling cold potatoes from the fridge, heating the pan and putting on another small pot. Soon the scent of fried onions and mushrooms, potatoes and searing steak filled the kitchen. In an amazingly short time, London set the plate in front of her with a rare steak, potatoes, onions and mushrooms and a serving of green peas.

"Do you mind if I have a glass of wine?"

"Superwoman deserves a glass of wine," Megan said as she cut the steak and shoved the first bite into her mouth. She moaned as she chewed and swallowed. "Delicious."

With her hunger appeased, the aches dissipated. She'd obviously overdone things today. Jacey was right, and she needed to slow down. She swallowed the last mouthful and pushed her plate away from her with a satisfied sigh. Another yawn escaped.

"Megan, go to bed. Even if you don't sleep straightaway, you need to relax and take things easy. Go," London ordered. "No one will mind if you have an early night."

"I think I might," Megan said, standing.

A quick shower took care of the rest of her muscle twinges and she slid between the sheets, intending to read more of Jacey's book about werewolf lore. She picked up where she'd left off. Werewolves could live for up to three hundred years. Hmm, difficult to hide in the modern age. Maybe her new series should start at a point where humans knew about mystical creatures. Her eyes grew heavy, and the words blurred. Finally, giving up, Megan set the book aside and gave in to her craving for sleep.

Jacey arrived home later than he'd expected. He'd made up his mind while running across the hills and playing chase with Henry and Gerard amongst the piles of schist covering the hillside. He'd tell Megan tonight, explain what he was and what it meant to their relationship. The longer he left it, the worse the potential outcome. He knew he wouldn't be forgiving if Megan kept a secret of this magnitude from him.

"Dinner smells good," Henry said as they neared the front door.

"I'm starving," Gerard said.

They piled in the doorway, dirty and sweaty but each of them content after their run. Jacey had felt the call of the moon tonight and the hard-out run had lessened the demand of the wolf. His wolf relaxed now, satisfied by the physical exertion.

London sat at the breakfast bar, engrossed by something on the tablet. His tablet, Jacey noted.

"Where is Megan?"

"She was tired, so I made her an early dinner and she went to bed. Why didn't you tell me she is Carrie English?"

Jacey halted. "She told you?"

"Yes, and I hired myself as her promo person," London said, lifting her chin.

"Megan is *the* Carrie English?" Gerard asked.

"The author? The one who writes those hot love scenes?" Henry demanded. "The ones Gerard reads to London for foreplay."

London slapped Henry on the arm. "Shush. Enough of that."

"The very one," Jacey said, proud of Megan's accomplishments.

"We're not allowed to tell anyone else," London said. "But Megan said it was okay if both of you knew."

"A lot of secrets around this place," Henry commented.

"There won't be for much longer," Jacey said. "I've decided to tell Megan everything."

"Pop, she writes paranormal romance. If anyone can accept feline shapeshifters and dragons, it is Megan."

Jacey agreed with London, not that it made spilling the truth any easier. "I'll check on Megan and take a quick shower."

"Dinner in ten minutes," London said.

Jacey nodded. "I'll be here on time."

When he entered their suite, Megan was sound asleep, her breathing low and even. At least she was a heavy sleeper. He padded into the en suite and took a shower to wash off the mud splatters from his run. Megan was still asleep when he left to join the kids for dinner.

SHE DREAMED OF WOLVES.

A pack of wolves, running through the darkness, singing to the moon.

Megan stood, watching them play and frolic. Itchiness fizzled across her arms and legs, envy at the wolves' carefree nature, their freedom, drawing her closer. She ached to run, the itchiness sinking to her bones.

She had to move. *Had to move.*

She forced her limbs to motion. A sudden fiery ache caused her breath to catch, a pained scream rushing forth. What was wrong with her? The niggles and twinges of earlier were nothing compared to this blazing agony. A roar burst up her throat, her entire body arching forward.

The wolves ran and ran, disappearing from her sight, and despite the pain tormenting her entire body, the craving to follow became even stronger.

Without warning, something burst inside her and she fell forward. A glance down at her arms tore a shriek from her. Excitement filled her as she realized she had turned wolfish.

She could run. She could play. She could howl at the moon.

CHAPTER FOURTEEN

JACEY SHUFFLED ON HIS chair at the dinner table, surreptitiously checked his watch. He had this urge to go to Megan, yet he didn't want to hover. She needed her space.

"Pop." London's sharp voice made him jump.

Gerard and Henry ceased their chatter about a quote for a job. Jacey had checked out of the conversation five minutes ago.

"What?"

"Check on Megan. It's obvious you want to. If she's awake, ask if she wants pudding. I made a lemon tart while I was waiting for you guys to come home for dinner."

Jacey sprang up without a second urging. Gerard made a mumbled comment to Henry, and they both sniggered, probably something at his expense. He didn't care. His wolf wanted to see Megan and reassure himself of her safety.

He shook his head. No wonder Henry and Gerard were poking fun at him.

The instant he opened the door to the suite, he smelled wolf. A strange scent yet familiar too. He froze, scanning the surroundings as he left the door open and stepped inside. Megan wasn't in the bed. Although his eyesight could pierce the dark of the room, he reached to the right to hit the switch because he wanted Megan to see him.

"Megan," he called.

A whine came from the far side of the bed.

"Megan?"

The figure uncurled, tipped back their head and let out a howl that lifted the hair at the back of his neck.

Fear stabbed at Jacey as he cautiously approached the bed to get a better look.

"Dad?" Henry stood in the open doorway with Gerard and London standing right behind him.

"Wait there," Jacey ordered, not taking his gaze off the howling figure. Blonde hair. Wolfish snout. The remains of a pink T-shirt clung to a fur-covered back and upper arms. "Hey. It's okay. Let me see."

Another panicked howl filled the room, and he wanted to howl in concert. Jacey tamped down his wolf and approached with care. Concern and shock thumped through him. Megan...no, it was impossible, but it was because he recognized her hair. Her scent. The mangled pink T-shirt.

"Careful, Dad. She's panicked."

Henry had come to the same conclusion as him. Somehow, Megan had shifted. Not a normal shift but a

221

half-shift, which took great skill and strength to hold. A werewolf who could do a partial shift was a rare being indeed.

"No, stay back there."

In his peripheral vision, Jacey saw London brush past Gerard, despite his objection.

"Careful, London. Her wolf is in control. She won't know what is happening to her."

"She won't hurt any of us," London said, coming even closer. "It was her choice to move to Middlemarch and change her life to be with you. She'll get past this."

Jacey's breath caught in his throat. He hoped London's confidence wasn't misplaced.

"We're sure that is Megan?" Gerard asked the obvious question.

"Who else could it be?" London tossed her head. "No one else could have entered with none of you noticing. Megan went to your suite, and I haven't seen her since, ergo this is Megan."

"Ergo?" Henry shook his head.

Megan held out her hands. Blonde fur covered her arms, and Jacey knew she'd make a beautiful wolf. She gave a garbled howl, her eyes—longer and more slanted than usual—full of distress.

"Shush, sweet pea," Jacey said. "It's okay."

Megan howled—the mournful cry sending gooseflesh over his arms.

"Tell her how to shift," London said. "She might not know. Did you do something to her to make her turn into a wolf?"

"No, of course not." Jacey had no idea that someone not full wolf could shift. If it had happened before, the stories hadn't reached him, and he'd been around a while. "Megan, close your eyes."

Megan stood and Jacey blinked in surprise. She darted past him and the others and out the door before he could marshal a protest.

London was the first to move. "Quick. After her before someone else sees her. Someone that shouldn't see her. What if those stupid reporters are loitering at our gate again?"

Jacey sprang after her with Henry and Gerard following. They burst outside just as Megan vaulted over the fence into a paddock.

"What the hell do we do?" Jacey watched Megan scurry across the grass, then stop to stare at the moon.

London folded her arms across her chest. "I suggest you and Henry shift and do whatever wolfies do during the full moon. She's not running away. She seems to want to run, and she's staring at the moon. It seems to mesmerize her."

London was right. Megan was acting moonstruck—like a wolf that hadn't shifted for a long time.

Jacey yanked at his clothes, stripping rapidly and almost falling flat on his face because of his haste.

London and Gerard sniggered until Gerard realized she was gawking at a naked male.

He growled. "Eyes front, mate."

Henry frowned in Megan's direction. "Are you sure you want me to help?"

"Yes. Yes. Hurry." Bloody hell. He should have told

Megan earlier, prepared her for the knowledge that werewolves existed. It might not have changed the outcome, but at least she'd have been prepared. The terror in her eyes had been like a blade to his chest. Stupid. So stupid. He needed his son's presence to make sure he didn't fuck up any worse than he had already.

Jacey pictured his wolf and his body flowed into his wolf shape. Black fur dipped in silver spread across his naked skin. He embraced the pain of the shift, thinking he deserved every bit of it for failing Megan. He dropped to his paws and turned to watch Megan. She scampered across the grass, and as he watched, she screeched to a halt, threw back her head and howled.

Thankfully not a full wolfish howl, but bad enough to attract the neighbors or unwanted visitors.

"Go to her," Gerard insisted, urgency in his tone.

Jacey took off, resolve thrumming in him now. If someone heard and came to investigate...

The Feline council had told him that several of the shifters opposed his and Henry's presence. They were in the minority, but if they screwed up...if someone heard Megan or saw her.

Henry ran behind him, and together, they took the fence, sailing through the air. His wolf delighted in the shift, thrilled at his mate scampering around the paddock. It was the man who feared the outcome.

Megan ran across the grass, the scents, the sounds, the crisp outlines of the trees and buildings almost too much for her senses to register. Sometimes on two legs. Sometimes hunched forward and using her hands—paws—for extra speed. The craving for motion kept her going, and she chased the dappled shadows rippling across the ground.

Faster. Faster. *Faster*.

It was exhilarating. It was freedom. *It was weird*.

This last thought caused her to stumble. She slowed and threw back her head to howl. It was as if she were two separate beings in the same body and she understood none of it. She gasped for breath, about to howl her anguish again when she caught sight of the moon.

Pretty. So big and bold in the sky.

She stared, spellbound by the beauty.

A new scent crept into her consciousness. Someone approached. She whirled around, sniffing, allowing her senses to catalog the risk of those advancing in her direction. The familiarity had her freezing in confusion. Two wolves approached. One mainly black with a silver belly and chest and the other a lighter brown. They stopped a few feet from her. Each stared at her, and she inwardly cringed at her appearance.

The part of her that wanted to run and play and enjoy the moonlight told her to take care. Make sure it was safe. They had to take care of their baby.

The thought propelled panic to the surface. A whimper escaped.

The black wolf whimpered in reply, the sound and his appearance digging at her memory.

The brown wolf lowered its front legs to the ground and bounced on his back legs. He yipped and bounded away,

225

only to repeat the movement.

Play. He wanted to play.

She yipped in return and chased, running past the black wolf to catch the brown one. The stranger controlling her actions thrilled at the invitation and yipped again in encouragement.

She chased the brown wolf around the paddock, going faster and faster until her sides heaved.

As they approached the black wolf, they slowed and the brown wolf trotted up to him, gave him a sharp nudge in the side with his nose.

Familiarity struck again, and her brain told her she knew these wolves. She scampered closer, drawing in their scents, and finally, her mind presented her with answers.

Jacey. Henry.

But no. That made little sense.

They weren't wolves.

The air seemed to distort around the black wolf. With the moon behind him, she couldn't help but stare. Such a beautiful wolf.

The shape of his body changed, transformed to...to...Jacey?

She blinked, her mouth gaping at her beautiful, naked man.

Jacey crouched in front of her. "Megan. Picture yourself as you look when you see your reflection in the mirror. Do it," he insisted when she continued to gape, tongue hanging out the side of her mouth.

A cloud skittered across the face of the moon, obscuring part of the pearly globe.

Aww. While she waited anxiously for the moon to reappear, the brown wolf approached her. He butted his head into her side, and she whirled with a snarl.

"Megan." Jacey's stern voice demanded attention.

She backed up and turned to face Jacey while keeping the brown wolf in her sight.

"Megan, picture your blonde hair, your pert nose, your blue eyes. Do it now."

Grumpy boots. But his words pierced through her brain and connected with the smaller, lessor being inside her. Her recollection swam into her mind and she grasped at it. Pain seeped into her consciousness, but the weaker being became stronger, determined, angry.

The vision of her appearance held, and with a whooshing pop, the weak became strong. Dominant.

Megan stared at a naked Jacey, stared at the brown wolf sitting nearby, stared at the tatters of her pink sleepshirt hanging from her body. She blinked. She swallowed as she replayed her memories.

Jacey sighed, his face appearing pale in the moonlight, although how she could see so well outside at night, she didn't know. Her vision had always been excellent, but not this good.

Scowling, she marched up to him, placed her hands on her hips and scowled, uncaring about wrinkles. "What the fuck just happened?"

CHAPTER FIFTEEN

"YOU'D BETTER COME INSIDE before you get cold," Jacey said, his heart knocking with nerves. "I'll explain everything inside." Megan didn't look happy. In fact, her distinct scowl cried pissed.

He gestured her in front of him and she marched, her shoulders rigid with good posture. Henry trotted past them, and Megan stumbled on seeing him.

Jacey raced forward and scooped her up before she could fall, his swift steps taking them to the house. He fumbled with the latch of the gate, not willing to risk jumping over with Megan in his arms.

"Why are you naked?"

Jacey sighed again as he struggled to think what to tell her. The truth, of course, but that didn't make this confession any easier.

London, seeing him try to juggle the gate, nudged Gerard, and the boy jogged over to open it for them.

"Shift," he heard London order Henry.

Jacey hesitated, wanting to shout in the negative. But London was right. A wise woman. Megan knew what had happened but her mind was struggling to put the facts in order.

Henry waited until they were through the gate and closer to him before he shifted to human.

Jacey heard Megan's swift intake of air, felt the growing tenseness of her muscles. She struggled within his arms, and Jacey let her down. She stepped away from him. He scanned her expression, and his heart stuttered. He wanted to touch her again, to embrace her, but her scowl told him she wouldn't welcome his advances.

"Henry, shift to wolf again," London ordered. "Gerard, you shift too."

Gerard nudged London with his hip. "She'll see my naked body."

"She's too busy staring at Henry," London said.

Gerard hesitated but at Jacey's curt nod, he disrobed and shifted. He stretched feline limbs and went to stand beside Henry. Henry slapped his tongue over Gerard's nose. London giggled as Gerard growled at his friend.

"What do you think of our two clowns?" London asked, her attention on Megan.

"You're not human," Megan intoned.

"I am human," London said. "Gerard is a feline shapeshifter. Henry and Jacey are werewolves. Many of Middlemarch's residents are feline shapeshifters. Henry and Jacey and now it seems, you, are the only werewolves in the community."

"I'm not a werewolf," Megan said. "Excuse me. I'm cold. I'm going to have a shower." Before any of them could reply, she marched inside.

Henry and Gerard both shifted and reclaimed their clothes. London handed Jacey his clothes, and he dressed too.

"I think you should call Gavin," Henry said. "He needs to make sure she is okay."

"I'll do it," London said, worry making her freckles stand out more. "Go and check on Megan. Call if you need me."

Megan stood under the shower, the warm water driving the chill from her limbs. Her mind ran in a tangled circle. She had...

Her rational brain refuted her explanation. But her mind hadn't played her false just now. Gerard and Henry had shifted to animals in front of her. A black leopard and a wolf. Jacey was a wolf too. She'd seen him transform. And she...

No.

Impossible.

"Megan?" Jacey appeared in the en suite.

"Why didn't you tell me?"

"I was afraid of losing you."

She snorted. "You had a prime opportunity to tell me when I told you about my writing. When you found me reading a book about wolves."

"I should have told you, but we haven't known each

other long. I worried about what you might say."

"We're having a baby." Oh, god. "Will our baby be a werewolf?"

Jacey swallowed. "I don't know. Normally, if a human and a werewolf produce offspring, the child can't shift. But you..." He shrugged, looking as miserable as she felt.

"Wait, you were in my cottage at Gilcrest Station. Why?"

Jacey hung his head and sighed. "Henry and I were running with Leo Mitchell. You took a photo of us, and we couldn't let you see it or send it to the media."

"But I didn't have any photos."

"You did." This time he met her accusing gaze. "Henry and I deleted them before you could see them."

"I see." She'd seen a terrier while she'd been out walking that day. Now she knew without asking, it had been Geoffrey since he followed Henry everywhere. "I want to talk to London."

"I—"

"I want to talk to London," Megan repeated.

Jacey gave a curt nod and retreated.

Megan turned off the shower and grabbed a towel. Her muscles felt tired, as if she'd run for miles, but the aches that had plagued her bones all day had disappeared. In the bedroom, she pulled on a long sleepshirt and clean panties.

A knock sounded and seconds later, the door opened. London stuck her head through the gap. "Can I come in?"

Megan gestured her inside.

"Gavin is on his way. He is the feline doctor," London said.

"I don't need a doctor."

"Maybe not," London said. "But you're seeing him. He's a good man and I can be here while he examines you. You changed to wolf." She wrinkled her nose. "Did a half change," she amended. "Don't you want to make sure your baby is okay?"

Megan's hand moved to her belly, the protective move not escaping London's notice.

"Very well." London was right. She wanted to know if her baby was all right and she could hardly go to a new doctor with tales of running around in the moonlight as an animal. A sob escaped. "Is there a spare room I can use for tonight?"

"There is a spare bedroom for guests, but are you sure? Jacey is distraught. He's blaming himself for not preparing you—"

"He knew this would happen?" Megan said at a near shriek. She'd gut the man.

"No, he didn't. None of us knew this was a possibility. But he's upset and worried about you."

Her hands clenched painfully hard at her sides, as she struggled to cope with her thoughts, her fear, the enormity of her discovery. "I'll sleep in the spare room."

"All right." London heaved an unhappy sigh.

A knock sounded.

"That will be Gavin."

Panic roared to life in Megan again. A tremor sped through her limbs. "Stay with me."

"Of course." London went to the door and opened it.

Megan glimpsed Jacey and turned away. She heard the soft murmur of London's voice before the door shut.

"Megan, this is Gavin Finley, our local vet."

Megan swung to face the man, expecting...she wasn't sure whom, but it wasn't the young man with piercing green eyes who stood in front of her, a leather bag in his left hand.

"I hear you've had quite an adventure tonight," he said with a smile. "Let's check you and your baby out. Do you have any pain? Any bleeding?"

Gavin set her at ease with his confident manner. His verdict. She and the baby were fine. She was in excellent health. He made an appointment for her to see him in a week and told her to ring him if she had any concerns at all.

"I told you he was nice," London said. "I use him as my doctor."

"But you're human."

"I'm mated to a feline shapeshifter, which makes my blood a little different. There are a few of us humans who are mated with felines."

"I'm tired," Megan said abruptly.

"Sure," London said. "Grab what you need, and I'll show you the room."

Once Megan collected toiletries, her phone and a change of clothes, London guided her along the passage and into a pretty bedroom with a double bed.

"You can use the bathroom two doors down," London said.

"Will you tell Jacey I want to be alone?"

"You should tell him yourself."

Megan grasped London's arm. "No, please. Just tell him

I want to think."

"Very well." Disapproval lined London's face. "I'll see you in the morning."

London appeared in the kitchen where Jacey sat with Henry and Gerard.

Jacey straightened. "Is Megan all right?"

"You spoke to Gavin?" A frown knit her brow, and Jacey heard what she wasn't saying. Something was very wrong.

Jacey clenched and unclenched his hands in his lap. "Yes, but how do you think she is?" Something in London's expression told him before she even answered.

"She is sleeping in the guest bedroom tonight. She wants to be alone to think."

A growl burst from Jacey, and London backed up a step.

"Dad." Henry placed a hand on his shoulder, and for once Jacey didn't take pleasure in the address. "This isn't London's fault."

"Sorry. I didn't mean to growl at you." Jacey picked up the whisky Gerard had poured for him earlier and tossed back the contents. "I'm angry at myself."

"Pop, this isn't your fault. Yes, you should have told Megan, but I get why you waited. You weren't to know she would shift. No one could have predicted that."

Jacey set down his glass and stood, unable to remain in one place. "But she's pushing me away."

"Give her time," London said. "She's just learned everything she writes about is true. It's a lot to wrap her head around." London grabbed his arm and tugged him

234

to a stop as he passed her. "Don't force a confrontation, Pop. Give her a chance to regroup. Let her come to you."

While he saw the sense in London's advice, going against his instinct to challenge Megan's fears took every scrap of his self-control. Another growl bled free.

"Jacey, how about we go for another run," Gerard suggested.

"You stay with London," Henry said, climbing off his barstool. "I'll go with Dad."

A run. Yeah, probably a good idea. No way could he settle or sleep, knowing Megan was so close.

"Running is a good idea. Let's go."

Jacey walked from the house with Henry and felt as if he were leaving his heart behind.

THE NEXT MORNING, JACEY'S body ached from all the running he and Henry had done the previous night with Saber, Leo and Felix Mitchell. They'd bunked at Saber's place. Now, he wanted to speak with Megan, to apologize and make things right. He pushed open the front door and sniffed the air. Scrambled eggs and sausages. He strode into the kitchen and found Gerard and London drinking coffee. Dirty plates sat in front of them, and London had trimmed the crusts off her toast as usual.

"Is Megan still asleep?"

Henry came into the kitchen after him and headed straight for the coffeepot. He poured two mugs and handed one to Jacey.

Gerard and London exchanged a glance, and his gut tightened with foreboding.

His hand curled around the coffee mug, the heat from the coffee blistering hot. "What?"

London sucked in a noisy breath. "Megan is gone."

His hand jerked and coffee splashed onto the counter. "Where?" he demanded hoarsely. "Where has she gone?"

"I can't tell you. I promised." London looked miserable.

"Is she coming back?"

"I don't know, but she promised she'd talk to you once she knew what she was doing. She intends to speak with you rather than sneaking off."

"I suppose I should be grateful." Bitterness sprang forth along with another growl.

"Don't growl at London," Gerard said. "This isn't her fault. She's balancing a line between you and Megan, and it's not fair to blame her for Megan's decision."

Jacey gave a curt nod. "Sorry."

"Pop, I tried to get her to change her mind. I really did. She's confused and still in shock. The pregnancy hormones can't be helping."

"She's safe?"

"Yes."

"And you won't tell me where she is?"

London averted her gaze. "I promised."

"All right. If she needs anything or wants to speak with me, let me know."

236

MEGAN WANDERED AROUND THE interior of the Stone Farm cottage at Gilcrest Station. A circuit of the open lounge and kitchenette, into the bedroom, back out and around again. She was staying in the same cottage as last time. Yet, this stay she found it hard to settle. A combination of restlessness and loneliness assailed her. Weird. As angry as she was at Jacey, she still missed his presence. Her mind darted from one subject to the next.

Werewolves were real.

She was a werewolf.

Jacey hadn't bitten her—well, he had, but he'd never broken the skin or made her bleed.

Fact: She'd always enjoyed a meat-rich diet, with rare meat her preference.

Fact: Her eyesight had always been better than average.

Fact: The previous evening she'd transformed into a wolf and every one of her senses had magnified.

Somehow, she bore wolf genes, yet her parents hadn't adopted her. Tessa showed none of the same signs as her, and neither did her parents. Wait, her mother liked to eat meat too. But, unless her parents were keeping secrets, neither of them turned wolfish and howled at the moon.

Fact: She seemed to have an affinity for the moon, which according to legend was also a wolfish thing. Her computer and cell phone were full of moon pictures—some she'd taken and some she'd collected from stock photo sites.

Fact: She was a werewolf or at least a strange version of one because her lower body had remained human.

Fact: Jacey and Henry had changed into wolves and seemed to enjoy running with her.

Fact: She'd glimpsed her reflection. Jacey's wolf, Henry's wolf—both gorgeous. She'd turned into something hideous. An abomination.

She traveled a circuit of the cabin, her mind struggling to keep up with her quick-fire thoughts. She had to get her crap together before Dillion Grieves arrived. When he'd called to let her know he had a window of three days, she'd jumped at the chance. Determined to do a good job, she ceased her pacing and stomped to a wooden coffee table where she'd dumped her notes.

What she had was a large number of facts with no background information.

A tap sounded on her cabin door. That had been quick...unless Jacey had tracked her down. No, London had promised. She jumped when a second, more impatient tap sounded. Only one way to find out. She strode to the door and yanked it open before she could second-guess herself.

Dillion Grieves—bad-boy country star—stood in front of her. "Good choice of hideaway," he said in his gritty voice. "Let's get to work. I need to be back in Wellington in three days. You have coffee? I've organized them to bring us lunch. You said you had questions for me? Let's do this."

Megan appreciated his no-nonsense attitude and the way he didn't flirt with her. "I hope lunch isn't salad. I like meat."

He stared at her and grinned without warning, taking his moody face to arresting and sexy. "I remember that from our dinner."

Megan made a pot of coffee, a cup of tea for herself,

and they started work. Her agent had warned her of his reputation as a perfectionist, his moods and his womanizing ways, yet he displayed none of that as he answered her questions and showed her photos of his childhood and days on the road and at gigs.

They continued after their break for lunch until Megan yawned.

"I'm sorry," she said finally and set down her pen. "This pregnancy makes me tired, and I seem to need an afternoon nap." She didn't mention she'd been awake half the night, howling at the moon.

"You should have said."

"Pregnancy isn't a disease. I can still write this book and do a good job."

"I didn't mean that." He stretched his arms above his head. "We can take breaks. There is no need to work nonstop."

"We're almost finished nutting out the chapter headings. Let's finish that before taking a break."

The tentative chapter headings took another half-hour.

Dillion stood and stretched again. "We've got through more than I thought we would. My agent wanted me to go with someone else who has a proven record, but I told him I thought you would be better. I was right."

Pleasure suffused her at the compliment. "Thanks."

"I'm going to drive to this town you told me about. Is it far?"

"Maybe ten minutes. Make sure you wear a disguise," Megan said. "There have been a few reporters hanging around, or at least there were. I think they've given up on me. If you want something to eat, the café does great food. I haven't visited the pub, but I hear it can be entertaining, and they sometimes do music on the weekends." She checked her watch. "School is out soon, so there will be lots of people around, collecting their kids."

Dillion nodded. "I know how to keep a low profile."

"They're used to tourists. If anyone asks, say you're doing the rail trail."

Once Dillion left, her mind returned to wolves. If she was going to turn into that hideous beast all the time, it was clear she couldn't return to the city. If what Jacey and the others said was true, Middlemarch was home to many supernatural beings. She pushed out a hard breath. If only she didn't feel so blindsided. If only she didn't look so ugly, so different. In this modern world, different got you attention, and she didn't want to stand out in the crowd.

Been there. Done that.

A process of elimination led Jacey to the cottages at Gilcrest Station. His wolf settled as soon as he spotted London's car parked at the side of the same cottage where Megan had stayed before.

She hadn't left Middlemarch.

Maybe he could fix this and persuade Megan to stay.

He took one step toward the cottage and stopped as he heard London's voice in his head. *Give her time to think.*

The thought gave him pause.

Megan hadn't left.

He backed away and returned to where he'd left Gerard's vehicle, tucked away in a concealed driveway.

"Where have you been?" Henry asked when he arrived

back at the house. "Gerard wanted his vehicle to do a job. He had to take mine." Geoffrey sat at Henry's side and cocked his head, as if he were listening to the conversation.

"Sorry." Jacey left it at that. "What do you need me to do next?"

"I've got two quotes for burglar alarms. People have been jumpy since that gang of thieves hit Middlemarch. Good for business. I'm fitting an alarm at a house as well. You can come with me. We can discuss what to do about Megan."

"What do you mean?" Jacey stiffened.

"I thought it wouldn't hurt to research her family tree as far as we can. It might help us work where her wolf blood came from. We should also try to learn as much as we can about half-shifting. You realize that if there are other humans out there who can shift in the same way as Megan, it will widen the gene pool. You and I have gone where our hearts led us, but some shifters will only mate with other shifters. This new knowledge will help all werewolves."

"Thanks. I meant to do some research earlier when I smelled wolf on Megan but got sidetracked with other stuff."

Jacey followed Henry to Gerard's vehicle. "You want to drive?"

Henry opened the driver's door and Geoffrey leapt inside the vehicle. "You can share your seat with Geoffrey. He likes to stick his head out the window."

Jacey rolled his eyes. "Don't we all."

By that evening, he and Henry had researched Megan's family tree back to her great-grandparents, thanks to

London's help and her discovery of a story written about Megan's background.

"Her mother's family come from Scandinavia," Jacey said. "I'd bet that is the link because her father's Scottish links don't go far back in the generations. I wonder if her younger sister has the same ability."

Henry tapped his chin. "It could be that the contact with other wolves and her becoming pregnant is the trigger. We need Megan's help to do more research on her family. We have to check that what we've discovered so far is correct because we've made a few assumptions. They could be wrong."

"What about the half-form?" Gerard asked. "I've never heard of felines doing a half-shift. How many wolves can do it?"

"Not many," Jacey said. "I've consulted all my research books. Only a few documented cases. Megan is a rarity."

"Did she see herself?" London asked and wrinkled her freckled nose. "She wasn't…um…there's no easy way to say this. She looked…uh…weird."

"Ugly," Henry supplied.

"To me she was just Megan," Jacey said.

London beamed at him. "You might tell her that, when you get the opportunity. A woman likes to hear her man thinks she is beautiful and gorgeous."

"Not only that," Jacey murmured, picturing Megan in his mind's eye. "She is my miracle."

By THE END OF her third day at the cottage, Megan felt as if she were climbing out of her skin. She said goodbye to Dillion, entered her cottage and drew the curtains even though it was still light. The moon pulled at her and the monstrous beast she'd caged at the back of her mind yammered and howled for release. Hot. Fire burned across her skin, and she yanked off her denim jacket.

Jacey. She wanted Jacey.

No! She'd been so ugly, and she'd slobbered when her stupid tongue kept flopping out of her mouth. How could Jacey want her knowing of the ugly beast that lived inside her?

Her vision shimmered, and she felt weird.

Without giving it a second thought, she picked up her phone and hit speed dial.

"Jacey." Her voice emerged in a guttural garble.

"Megan?"

"Help me." She fumbled the phone as pain shot down her arm. In front of her horrified gaze, blonde fur rippled down her forearm. Fingertips morphed into claws and the phone clattered to the floor.

Her T-shirt and bra strained against the changes of her upper body. She felt her face creak and crack and change shape. Her eyesight sharpened, and she moaned at the jagged pain. She curled into a ball and shut her eyes, willing the being in her brain—the howling, slobbering being—to go away.

"What is it?" Henry demanded.

243

"Megan." Jacey snatched Gerard's keys off the counter in the kitchen and took off at a run.

"Wait for me," Henry snapped.

London slid off her barstool. "Gerard. We're going too."

They piled into the vehicle, Geoffrey squeezing in beside Henry in the passenger seat. Gerard hadn't even shut the rear door before Jacey took off.

"How do you know where she is?" London demanded as they screeched down country roads. "You'd better pray that Laura or Charlie aren't patrolling the roads. They're having a drunk driver campaign at present."

"I used the process of deduction," Jacey snapped.

The drive to Gilcrest Station took less time than normal, and they entered the code to the main security gates a short time later. The SUV screeched to a halt in front of the cottage, and Jacey jumped out. He sprinted to the cottage door and flung it open, thankful to find it unlocked.

He sniffed and followed his nose into the bedroom. Megan huddled in the far corner of the bedroom, away from the windows. He skidded to a halt by her side, his heart breaking when he saw her shuddering body.

"Megan, sweet pea. I'm so glad to see you."

She turned her head toward him and whimpered.

He wrapped his arms around her, the physical contact relaxing his own wolf. He pressed her large wolf head to his chest and kissed the side of her furry face. His miracle.

Gradually, her trembling faded. He continued to murmur comforting words and press kisses to her face, her ears, her snout.

"Pop, maybe Megan might like to try shifting back to

CHAPTER SIXTEEN

LATER THAT NIGHT

"So you're saying I have werewolf ancestors?" Megan asked.

She lay in Jacey's king-size bed, with Jacey's naked body pressed to hers.

"Yes. I smelled the wolf in you when we met. It confused me, but it has become stronger since you became pregnant."

Megan thought about her family. Her mother. Her grandfather. "My mother eats a lot of meat, and from memory my grandfather did too. My sister, Tessa, wears glasses for reading while my vision has always been excellent."

"What about your mother's brothers and sisters?"

"She was an only child."

"We think your wolf blood comes from your mother's side. Your mother married a human, which should dilute the bloodline further, but somehow, you have received the gene while it appears your sister hasn't. Most people wouldn't meet a wolf or make love to one. Ah, there is something I didn't tell you. You know when the condom broke?"

"Yes."

"Somehow, my cock extended a type of barb. It held us together, but you didn't seem to notice."

"I noticed the incredible sex. I don't think I've ever come so hard. I think I left my body."

"Anyhow, that is how you became pregnant."

Megan considered this. "Our wolf sides taking control."

"Yes."

"Any other secrets I should know?"

"You know everything I do now," Jacey said. "You know what I'd like to do now?"

"What?"

"Make love to you and make you my mate."

"How do you do that?"

He patted the fleshy part of her shoulder where it met her neck. "I bite you here, and you do the same to me. It mingles our blood and we become mates. You'll feel an invisible tie between us, have a better instinct for what I'm feeling."

"But I'm an ugly freak."

"Not to me. You'll understand how much I love you once the mating ties snap into place. And I love you. Your half-form is rare and was much revered during early centuries."

"Why?" She couldn't for the life of her think why.

"The shift is quicker and the half-form—the ability to stand—strengthens you and is less vulnerable. From what I've read, you should be able to finesse your shifts and shift just one arm if you want. A quick weapon during times of war."

"If you say so," she said, pulling a face.

"You enjoy running under a full moon. It's something we can share. We can shift most days, so the moon won't hold as much power over you. Regular shifts mean you can still travel and do everything you used to do. You'll gain control."

"I guess." He sounded so confident, his voice earnest as he told her he loved her. He'd kissed her ugly face, held and comforted her.

"I crave your body, your touch," he whispered in her ear. "Please be mine."

"Yes." She wriggled closer, both parts of her psyche telling her Jacey spoke the truth. He loved and wanted her.

Their lips met and her nostrils flared at the deeper scent of wolf. His hand lowered to cup her breast and heat flowed from her nipple, settled between her thighs. He kissed her again, this kiss designed to inflame and consume as he plundered her mouth. His erection strained against her hip and she pressed into it, suddenly desperate for the intimacy—the joining of two wolves. His hands roved her body, and she explored in return, her control dissipating from his first kiss.

He knew all her sensitive spots, and he used this knowledge to ramp up her desire until she trembled in his arms. Megan twisted against his body, urgency thrumming through her.

"Jacey," she wailed when he continued to kiss and stroke instead of fulfilling the erotic promise he'd stoked inside her.

"This isn't a race."

"I'm burning for you." She jumped as his tongue licked over the spot he'd told her he intended to mark. Maybe, just maybe...

She slanted her head and nipped the fleshy spot on him. His guttural groan raised a grin. Satisfaction. Raw, male desire pressed into her. She realigned their bodies, and they both moaned in pleasure as his thick cock pushed into her, filling the emptiness. Lust lanced through her body, and she kissed the mating spot on his upper shoulder. Instinct told her to bite, so she did. A primal sense of satisfaction swamped her as she felt his need.

Jacey surged into her, pulled free and thrust home again, his big body shuddering as she licked across the bite.

"God, Megan." Such feeling in his voice. It made her lightheaded with happiness.

Right now, she had no idea why she'd hesitated to get to this point. He accepted her. He saw her. Jacey loved her, and she returned the sentiment.

He pulled back again and plunged deep, the stimulation against her clit thrusting her into a maelstrom of pleasure that curled her toes. Jacey nuzzled her neck and entered her again. He bit down as he stroked into her. A flash of pain tore through her, but Jacey somehow knew and he slid a hand between them and rubbed her clit in the perfect way. The pleasure swelled again, the discomfort dispersing as he rocked into her, then stilled, his cock jerking as she luxuriated in the aftershocks.

Every sense thrilled to the moment. She cataloged the rich tapestry of scents and gloried to his hoarse breathing, the thud, thud, thud of Jacey's pulse. Her eyes, which she didn't remember closing, flicked open to see Jacey grinning down at her.

"How you doing, sweet pea?"

"I feel great. Different," she decided.

"You're my mate."

"I know. I feel the ties you mentioned. I didn't understand, but I do now." She reached up to cup his cheek. "You know, my sister told me I was silly to concentrate on a career after Charlie died. She said I'd regret it and end up alone. She didn't know I had a Plan B and was waiting for you."

"Hate to say it but your sister sounds like a bitch," Jacey said in a mild tone.

Megan laughed. "She can be, but my brother-in-law keeps her in check. She doesn't approve of me being pregnant at my age."

"Ah, but you have wolf genes. We age much slower than humans."

"You do? I will?"

"I think so," Jacey said. "We'll keep up our research to learn more about your background, and I can put out feelers to the pack in Perth. We'll learn more, but it will take time."

"It's okay," she said and kissed the tip of his nose. "It—I was scared at first, but knowing I'm not alone makes it easier."

"Henry and I will help you as much as you want, help you learn about your wolf. You can talk to Gerard or any of the Mitchell family. Gavin Finley. You can trust them to help if you feel out of control."

The caring in his tone tightened her chest with emotion. She had been so lucky to find Jacey. Plan B had some interesting repercussions when all the time she'd thought moving on had been a disaster.

"I love you, Jacey Anderson. Thank you."

"I knew where you were."

She grinned. "I figured that, but you still gave me space and I appreciate your patience." She drew his head down for another kiss, happier than she could ever remember. When she'd thought her life was over because she'd lost the job she coveted, all she'd needed was to follow her heart with plan B. She laughed and it was full of joy. Nothing wrong with plan B at all.

Bonus Chapter

Mitchell Farm, Middlemarch, New Zealand

Feline Shapeshifter Council Meeting.

Present: Sid Blackburn, Agnes Paisley, Valerie McClintock, Benjamin Urquart, Saber Mitchell

Saber Mitchell studied the chair where Kenneth Nesbitt usually sat and hesitated. Should he take it away before the council members arrived for the meeting, or should he leave the empty chair there in memory of the man who had recently died?

Emily would know what to do, but she'd taken herself off to the café since she was feeling better this week, the morning sickness having taken a break. He grinned as he pictured his mate's curvy body with her swollen belly.

She had never looked so beautiful. He glanced at his wristwatch. Maybe he had time to ring—

The doorbell interrupted that thought. Too late to move the chair now. It stayed in place. He flicked on the coffeemaker as he strode past to greet his visitors.

Sid Blackburn stood on the other side of the door, his thin white hair shifting in the blast of the wind. "Nasty weather today, lad. Some snow on the way, I think."

"It's cold enough," Saber said. "Come in. The coffee is on."

"Agnes rang to say they're on their way. She's picking up Ben and Valerie."

"Ah, lad." Sid came to an abrupt halt in the kitchen, his sight in line with the table in the dining room where they held their meetings. "You left Kenneth's chair in place."

"Should...should I move it? I wasn't sure."

Tears swamped Sid's eyes as he turned to Saber. "No, it's perfect as it is. We kept a chair for Herbert for a long time."

Saber gave a clipped nod and placed a plate of blueberry-and-white-chocolate muffins on the table. He still missed his uncle. "Uncle Herbert would have liked the way things are going in Middlemarch."

"Aye, lad, you have the right of it."

They both cocked their heads on hearing a car.

"That will be the others," Sid said. "I'll let them in."

Saber watched Sid amble from the kitchen. He'd noticed Sid, and the others looked their age at present. Kenneth's sudden death had shocked them, left them aware of their own vulnerability.

"Ah, good." Agnes bustled inside and shed her

green-tartan woolen coat. "You have the heater on. Think it will snow tonight."

"You left Kenneth's chair." Valerie's glasses fogged up, and she whipped them off to wipe the lenses with brisk wipes of a clean hanky.

"I...yes. Shall we start the meeting?"

They settled around the table, chatted and devoured Emily's muffins while Saber distributed mugs of coffee.

"The Sevens tournament went well, and thanks to Megan Saxon, we made a good profit on the gate," Agnes said with a glance at her notebook.

"It was a good weekend," Saber agreed. "Sly and Joe said all the players enjoyed the tournament. We mentioned making it an annual event. We should. It makes an excellent memorial for Kenneth."

"I agree." Ben tapped his fingers on the white tablecloth. "I think everyone enjoyed the weekend. Rumor says that Megan Saxon is moving to Middlemarch."

"Rumor would be right," Saber said. "She and Jacey Anderson are involved." He paused and decided the council members should know the truth. "Jacey told me Megan is a werewolf, so that makes three in our community. He asked me to keep it quiet since Megan didn't know she had werewolf blood and is still getting used to the fact."

"Interesting." Agnes cocked her head. "Must have come as a shock. I like the woman. She didn't give herself airs and worked hard during the tournament. I like Jacey too. The man is a gentleman."

High praise from Agnes, and the others must have

agreed because they nodded like a row of clowns at the A & P sideshow. "What's next on our agenda?" Saber asked.

"There's no point arranging anything until the spring," Valerie said. "Why don't we hold a spring picnic and have our contest for decorative bras." She winked at Agnes. "T-shirts optional." While Agnes cackled, Valerie continued, ticking off items on her fingers. "Egg and spoon races, sack races and a treasure hunt for the kids. Maybe a scavenger hunt for the adults. Lolly scramble. All traditional New Zealand favorites."

"How about the single ladies bring a lunch basket to be raffled off and the gentlemen can bid for the basket and the pleasure of the lady's company for lunch?" Ben suggested. "We used to do that when we were younger, remember?"

Agnes jotted down the ideas. "Gumboot throwing contest? For all ages." At their nods, she added it to her list.

Saber leaned back in his chair. "When should we hold the picnic? When does daylight saving start this year? Late September?"

Valerie consulted the calendar in her diary. "Third Sunday in September. How about the first weekend in October? If the spring weather looks iffy, we'll move the date to the following weekend. Everyone agreed? Okay. We can take our time with the arrangements. I'll liaise with London to design posters to put up in the town."

"Maybe do a separate one for the lunch baskets," Saber suggested. "We might need to nudge the single ladies. Let's make the idea more modern. If any of the single men want to offer a basket, the ladies can bid for those."

"That should make things interesting." Sid nodded his

approval. "You can work on Joe and Sly. The young ladies would bid like crazy for their baskets."

"They'd be wise not to eat their cooking," Saber said drily. "Emily despairs of those two."

Sid barked out a laugh. "A modern twist is a good idea, lad. Is that all? I'd like to get home before the weather turns for the worse."

"There is one more thing we need to discuss," Agnes said, and Saber heard clear hesitation, which made him pay attention. "I think we need to replace Kenneth on the council. I know it hasn't been long, but we need the help now that we're organizing more projects. Any suggestions about whom to appoint?"

Ben scratched his head. "We could put it to the vote at the next general feline shapeshifter meeting."

"Bah!" Valerie slashed her hand through the air. "Remember the kafuffle when Herbert died? Everyone wanted to be on the council, and when they found out they had to work, they changed their tune."

Saber remained silent since he was the youngest on the council. Best to let them slug it out regarding Kenneth's replacement.

Agnes shut her notebook with a snap. "I have a suggestion." She glanced at all their faces, waiting for comments.

"Who?" Saber spoke for all of them.

"I think we need someone younger. My vote is for London Allbright. She's young, intelligent, and understands modern technology. She's popular and everyone I've spoken to mentions her integrity."

Saber considered the suggestion, surprised by Agnes's vote for London since she was human, but approving of the appointment. "She is a hard worker. I like her, and so does Emily. Now that there are more human mates, it would make sense to have them represented on the council."

"What about the anti-human sentiments we've been hearing whispers of lately?" Ben asked.

"Huh!" Valerie lifted her nose in the air. "They're all mouth and no trousers. I wouldn't worry about them."

"All right," Sid said. "Let's vote. A show of hands. Who wants to appoint London to the Feline council?"

Saber raised his hand, as did everyone else on the council.

"Motion passed," Sid said. "That was an excellent idea, Agnes. Who wants to approach London?"

"Valerie and I will," Agnes said. "I need to speak with London about the posters, anyway. Do you want to approve them or should I get them printed and put them up at the beginning of September?"

"Go ahead with the printing," Sid said. "You and Valerie know the type of thing we want. Any other business?"

"No, that's it for today," Agnes said. "Saber, how is Emily? Is she still suffering from bad morning sickness?"

"It's been better this week. Dry toast and tea before she moves from bed seems to help."

"Boy or girl?" Valerie asked.

"Neither of us mind which sex we have. We told Gavin we didn't want to know." Saber smiled. "Gavin says Emily and the baby are healthy. The baby should kick soon."

"Hmm," Agnes said, standing. "I'm not sure whether I

wish you a mischievous boy or a sweet little girl. It will be fun watching you with your child. I'm kind of hoping for a little payback. I *know* it was you who raided my apple tree the day before I wanted to bake apple pies for the show."

"You have no proof of that." Saber met Agnes's narrow-eyed gaze for a good length of time.

"My apple tree was stripped bare."

Sid chuckled. "If I remember clearly, there were other suspects."

"Tell London that if she has any questions she can ask me," Saber said.

Ben nudged him in the ribs. "Good change of subject," he whispered.

"You know, I think we should mention at the next meeting that we're considering who to appoint to the empty council seat. Ask anyone interested to send in a submission, but we'll also lay out the expectations and duties of the new council member," Ben said. "Make it sound like hard work. We should also make sure that human mates are present, so when we announce London's appointment, everyone will think she made an application."

There was a lengthy silence. Saber started to grin, and he realized the other council members echoed his admiration and acceptance of Ben's suggestion.

"I am in awe of your sneakiness." Agnes stood and bowed in Ben's direction, making them all chortle.

"Who do you think told Saber and his friends about your delicious apples?" Sid asked.

"Traitor," Ben said, but his lips quirked. "Actually,

Kenneth was in cahoots."

Agnes shook her head and *tsk-tsked*. She turned a fraction to face Valerie, but Saber saw her quick wink. "They're all small boys at heart."

Valerie made a tutting sound. "I don't know why we put up with them. Ben, you and Sid can provide our refreshments for the next meeting. We'll hold it at the café."

Valerie and Agnes headed for the door, leaving Sid and Ben gaping at each other with wide eyes, as if to say, *How did that happen?*

"Sid, can you give me a lift? I don't know if I can bear riding with those two she-cats. They'll sharpen their claws on me all the way home."

Sid shuddered. "Don't blame you one bit. Thank you, lad. I guess we'll see you at the next meeting."

"At the café," Saber said, managing to keep a straight face. *Just*. He walked the two men outside and waved goodbye to the women. Laughter exploded from him, and he realized the meeting he'd dreaded hadn't turned out so bad. Kenneth remained with them in spirit as did Uncle Herbert. He couldn't wait to tell Emily about the apple saga.

It was true. Laughter was the very best medicine.

TIGERS ARE COMING TO country town Middlemarch! Turn the page for a glimpse of *My Cat Nap*, the next story in my Middlemarch Shifters series.

Shelley

EXCERPT – MY CAT NAP

MIDDLEMARCH SHIFTERS, BOOK 12

"Rohan, you have to come right now!" Ambar skated to a halt in the doorway of their West Auckland grocery store and stared at his customer in consternation. "Um hello, Mrs. McPherson," his sister said. "How are you?"

"Was there anything else you needed today, Mrs. McPherson?" Rohan Patel asked, ignoring Ambar's dramatic arrival. Their parents had believed in excellent customer service and enforced the principle with their children until it became second nature.

"No, thank you, dear," the elderly lady said. "How much do I owe you?"

"Ten dollars and twenty cents," Rohan answered, and waited for her to dig misshapen hands deep into her cloth bag to find her purse. Ever since he could remember, the elderly lady had shopped at his parents' store. Both he and Ambar had practiced waiting on her until they'd perfected the standard of service his parents expected. In his peripheral vision, he noticed Ambar's frantic gesturing and frowned, the training of years hard to shake.

"I'll miss you when you leave. Where did you say you were going?" Mrs. McPherson asked.

"Ambar and I have purchased a business in the South Island, a place in Middlemarch." Rohan couldn't wait to move to the country with all the open land, the mountains and the freedom to run during their leisure time. It would be great to have the sign above their new store bearing their names instead of their parents, to know they worked for themselves.

"It won't be the same without you. Your parents were lovely. I suppose it must be difficult without them?"

"Yes, it is hard, which is why we decided to start again in fresh surroundings. Ambar will help you carry your shopping out to your car," Rohan said, frowning at Ambar in clear displeasure, his older-brother-knows-best face in place. This was still their parents' store even if they owned it on paper now.

Ambar's eyes narrowed. "But—"

"Ambar." Rohan's voice held a warning, and the faint tensing of her shoulders told him she'd received the threat. Customers came first. Always. Their parents' philosophy drummed into them over the years was the reason the store remained popular with the locals.

Rohan watched Ambar tamp down her frustration. She nodded and picked up Mrs. McPherson's two bags of purchases. Silently she held the door open and waited for the woman to lumber through, the tap of her walking stick on the floor and pavement outside marking her unsteady progress. The second the car door closed after the elderly woman, Ambar darted back into the store. She flipped the lock and put the *Back in ten minutes* sign in the window.

"Rohan we have to hurry. I saw another shifter. He was hurt, and they put him into an ambulance."

Alarm shot through Rohan. "Hell, why didn't you say so?" A shifter helpless in human hands, even if they meant well, could spell disaster. The last thing any feline wanted was a life of imprisonment and intrusive study.

Ambar sniffed and rolled her golden-brown eyes. "You didn't give me a chance."

"Do you know where they're taking him?"

"Auckland Hospital. What are we going to do?"

Rohan grabbed his wallet. "I don't know, but we can't let them do tests on him. What sort of shifter?"

"Tiger, I think, although I'm not one hundred percent sure. He was big enough. It all happened so quickly I didn't have a chance to scent him properly. He looked out of it. Before they shut the ambulance doors, he opened his eyes. I don't think anyone else saw his eyes shift except me."

Rohan hurried through the store, past the jams and breakfast cereals aisle, to the rear door. "We're the only tigers around here. Most of them live over on the north shore. Are you sure?"

"I'm not sure of anything. As I said, it was over in minutes. Maybe I'm mistaken because his skin was lighter than ours." Ambar snatched her car keys from the top of the desk in their small office as she passed. "We can discuss this once we have him safe. You know what will happen when his test results come back from the lab." She thrust the keys at her brother. "You drive. You're faster than me."

They hurried out the rear exit, locking the door after them. Rohan yanked open the car door and jumped behind the wheel.

"I can't believe you're letting me drive," Rohan said, lips quirking in silent laughter while he pulled out onto the main road.

"Just hurry. You didn't see him. I did. I wouldn't wish admittance to a public hospital on any shifter." She shuddered, and Rohan could see her mind leaping to all sorts of scenarios. "We need to come up with a plan."

"You realize I'll give you a hard time if this turns out to be a waste of time."

"I don't care," Ambar retorted. "At least this way I can live with my conscience. I'd never forgive myself if I let a fellow shifter suffer—" She slapped her hand against the dashboard to catch herself as Rohan skidded around a corner. "Go easy. The last thing we need is a cop stopping us for speeding."

Rohan heeded the warning, slowing a fraction but still driving over the speed limit. They reached the hospital and spent fifteen frustrating minutes looking for parking. Finally they found a spot and hurried into the emergency department.

"How are we going to handle this?" Ambar whispered before they neared the desk.

"Let me do the talking," Rohan said. "And start thinking about JoJo."

Ambar drew a sharp breath, tears filling her eyes when

he mentioned her beloved cat. Jojo had died of old age at the end of last year, only weeks after their parents lost their lives in a fatal car crash. "Jojo?"

"Perfect," Rohan said. "Excuse me. We've just heard our brother Jojo was hurt in some sort of an accident. Can we see him?"

A sob escaped Ambar, and Rohan felt a flicker of guilt for using her in this way. She'd loved that cat. It had taken a long time for her to gain Jojo's trust because he'd sensed their shifter genes. Rohan would have given up but Ambar hadn't.

"What is his surname?"

"Jojo Patel," Rohan said smoothly. "Although he might not know his name. He has blackouts sometimes. He's tall like us. He takes after our mother and his skin is fairer." Rohan crossed his fingers and hoped the stranger really was tall.

"Let me check," she said, picking up a phone.

Ambar sniffed and shot him a quick look of approval for his fast thinking. Rohan hid a grin because, initially after their parents' death, they'd argued about moving from the city to the country. She'd told him he was dim-witted with no original thoughts to rub together inside his head. Leave the thinking to her because she did a better job.

Luckily, after more discussion she'd come to accept their move to Middlemarch wasn't such a bad one. Personally, he thought it was the large male-female ratio in Middlemarch that had swung Ambar's decision from negative to positive. Rohan had argued they needed to start over and living amongst other shifters would be a great start. There were too many of their parents' friends in Auckland who would judge them and try to offer unwanted advice.

Besides, Rohan had heard people in Middlemarch were more liberal when it came to same-sex relationships. He might even find the guts to admit his liking for males to his sister. A true fresh start. It would be good running through the countryside on a regular basis instead of slinking around in the dark of Western Springs reserve when the need to shift became too much for them. Good thing they were now on the same page.

"You can go through," the woman said. "The nurse will show you the way." She picked up a chart, and called, "Mr. James, you can go with the nurse."

They waited for the patient to follow the nurse before trailing them. Rohan sensed the uneasiness in his sister, the same tension lurking inside him. The smells and the sounds of the hospital were full of despair, the atmosphere sorrowful and downright depressing. This was dangerous. They both knew it, yet neither of them considered turning away from a fellow shifter in need.

Want to know what happens next? Read more about My Cat Nap at my website. (www.shelleymunro.com/books/my-cat-nap)

ABOUT AUTHOR

USA Today bestselling author Shelley Munro lives in Auckland, the City of Sails, with her husband and a cheeky Jack Russell/mystery breed dog.

Typical New Zealanders, Shelley and her husband left home for their big OE soon after they married (translation of New Zealand speak - big overseas experience). A twelve-month-long adventure lengthened to six years of roaming the world. Enduring memories include being almost sat on by a mountain gorilla in Rwanda, lazing on white sandy beaches in India, whale watching in Alaska, searching for leprechauns in Ireland, and dealing with ghosts in an English pub.

While travel is still a big attraction, these days Shelley is most likely found in front of her computer following another love - that of writing stories of contemporary and paranormal romance and adventure. Other interests include watching rugby (strictly for research purposes), cycling, playing croquet and the ukelele, and curling up with an enjoyable book.

Visit Shelley at her Website
www.shelleymunro.com

Join Shelley's Newsletter
www.shelleymunro.com/newsletter

ALSO BY SHELLEY

Paranormal

Middlemarch Shifters
My Scarlet Woman
My Younger Lover
My Peeping Tom
My Assassin
My Estranged Lover
My Feline Protector
My Determined Suitor
My Cat Burglar
My Stray Cat
My Second Chance
My Plan B
My Cat Nap
My Romantic Tangle
My Blue Lady

MY PLAN B

My Twin Trouble
My Precious Gift

Middlemarch Gathering
My Highland Mate
My Highland Fling

Middlemarch Capture
Snared by Saber
Favored by Felix
Lost with Leo
Spellbound with Sly
Journey with Joe
Star-Crossed with Scarlett

Lightning Source UK Ltd.
Milton Keynes UK
UKHW041006010323
417851UK00004B/251